SHOW OFF

SERAPH'S BURLESQUE CLUB

RENÉE DAHLIA

Print ISBN: 978-0-6489626-5-6

Cover Design: Sarah Paige of Opium House Creatives

Editor: Lauren Masson-Oakden

SHOW OFF

RENÉE DAHLIA

From casual hook up … to something more?

Burlesque dancer Charlie Kent should be happy performing and hooking up with sexy people now the pandemic is over, just like before. Instead it feels empty. The audience is always missing Elle, her friend-with-benefits. They were just casual, but Charlie now realises she wants more. Much more. When Elle arrives at the Seraph's Burlesque Club for business only, Charlie is not going to let this second chance go to waste.

Elle's interior design business has boomed since the pandemic with so much work she's barely thought of the sexy-as-sin burlesque dancer who she used to hook up with… Except when she's lonely all night. But she can't be just friends anymore, so she stays away. When she is commissioned to refit Seraph's Burlesque Club, Elle bumps into Charlie, and all her best intentions go out of the perfectly dressed window.

Elle must keep her professional reputation intact, and can't allow her attraction to Charlie to derail her work and her need for love. . . Unless she can have it all?

- friends with benefits to lovers
- second chances

ABOUT THE AUTHOR

Renée Dahlia is an unabashed romance reader who loves feisty women and strong, clever men. Her books reflect this, with a side note of awkward humour. Renée has a science degree in physics. When not distracted by the characters fighting for attention in her brain, she works in the horse-racing industry doing data analysis and writing magazine articles. When she isn't reading or writing, Renée spends her time with her partner and four children, usually watching them play cricket.

*To everyone who got vaccinated for COVID
as soon as they were eligible.*

FOREWORD

Welcome to SHOW OFF, the second book in the Seraph's Burlesque Club series.

This series consists of three lesbian romances is set in a burlesque club in London. If you love to read about a found family with queer people who thrive, this series has that and more. This book is friends (with benefits) to lovers with a high heat level.

Please note that this book is set in a post-COVID London where people are (mostly) vaccinated. There will be some references to the pandemic. There are also references to a character having long covid, parental fat shaming of a main character, parental manipulation, and a broken arm.

If you are keen to keep up to date on new releases and, more importantly, sales, I recommend you sign up to my newsletter, or follow me on social media or at romance.com.au

I hope you enjoy reading this book!
Renée

PROLOGUE

The burlesque dancer plucked Elle's glass of champagne from her hand and twirled away from her. Her tightly laced corset emphasised her slender waist and her breasts spilled enticingly over the top. From an aesthetic point of view, Elle was intrigued when she really didn't want to be. What exactly was feminist about dancing semi-naked for an audience? Elle rolled her eyes at the display, still unsure why her soon-to-be sister-in-law Willow had allowed her bridesmaids to bring them all to Seraph's Burlesque Club for her hens' party. And now her drink—the only thing keeping her from boredom—had been stolen by a glorious tall white woman stripping out of a Belle Epoque gown. The gown fell from her hips finishing just above the dancer's narrow ankles and bare feet. Okay, perhaps she wasn't precisely bored watching this dancer flirt with the audience. She was beautiful, in a disconnected aesthetic way, and so confident as she fluttered her feathers and shook her tits.

Elle glanced around the room again. The room had a theatrical quality with dim lights over the audience, and tables squeezed together. People leaned on the bar, men with shirt sleeves rolled up, and women in nice dresses, as the dancer moved under shining spotlights on the stage. Red curtains hung on either side of the stage, with gold tassels occasionally catching a glint of light. The stage was largely unadorned apart from the dancer who twirled and shimmied to music being played by a small jazz band at the side of the stage. Elle's glass of champagne had been placed on a chair in the centre of the stage; the whole set up really needed something more. Nothing that would detract from the dancer, but a little more care in the set design would make the experience better, more lush, for the audience. She couldn't help but use her design training to assess a room, and the stage here was no different.

Aside from Willow and her squealing friends, most of the audience were straight-passing couples. She scoffed at herself and her judgemental nonsense. She'd been part of a relationship like that and had hated the erasure from everyone who assumed she was straight just because she'd happened to have been fucking a man at the time. But damn, some of these men were salivating too openly at the dancer, while their wives looked as bored as she felt. She ought to wave at the waiter to get another drink. Bloody cheeky of the dancer to nick her champagne like that.

The dancer crouched on stage, right in front of Elle, and once again she cursed Willow under her breath for paying for a table next to the stage. The stage was level with her table, lower than Elle had expected when she'd first walked into the room. It brought an intimacy to the room that Elle appreciated even if she wasn't sure she wanted to be in the spotlight like this. Everyone must be staring at them now and she ignored the urge to wipe her face in case she had a crumb on her chin from the cheese platter they were sharing.

The dancer slowly dragged her gown up her leg, exposing lightly tanned silky bare flesh. Elle swallowed. That was an effective way to get rid of boredom. Elle gaped at the dancer, and the rest of the audience faded away. She was unable to look away, desperate for the glimpse into the shadows of the dancer's thighs. Salty sweat and the tiniest hint of a rose-based perfume filled her nostrils. Rose was one of her favourite scents; she didn't wear it herself as it made her feel like a grandmother, but she adored the heady fragrance of walking through a rose garden in summer.

Somehow, the dancer balanced on one leg and lifted her exposed leg, so her big toe rested on Elle's lip. A sensual shock jolted into her lungs, searing her breath. And when the dancer poured Elle's champagne down her leg so it dribbled into Elle's mouth, it was the hottest thing she'd ever experienced.

Elle's tongue chased the drops of liquid as it ran down the dancer's toe and onto her lips. She was so wet—instantly hot and ready—she was sure she was leaving a puddle on the chair. The dancer winked at her, then removed her leg, and spun away. For the rest of the performance, Elle couldn't move. She just sat there, her pulse racing, and her finger resting on her bottom lip. Now she understood why people came to watch burlesque.

She tracked the dancer across the stage, with every movement branded on her memory. When the dancer undid her skirt and it fell to the stage, Elle was once again reminded of roses, and when the dancer removed her corset to reveal perky tits with red tassels over her nipples, Elle was pretty sure she had stopped breathing completely. A little shake from the dancer sent a shiver down her spine. Her mouth dried and she almost licked her lips.

"Having fun?" Willow nudged her. "Isn't this so cool? Those ladies are so brave, getting up there. You'd never see me doing that."

"Um, yeah." Elle couldn't form words. She wiped her palms on her skirt, uncaring if the sheen of sweat would leave a mark on the fine fabric.

"I'm so glad you came along. I really want to be friends with you." Willow's drunken happiness came right as the dancer bent over and shook her almost naked bottom at Elle.

"Yeah."

Willow's squeal and rapidly spoken something didn't compute and Elle tried to nod politely at her. She couldn't look away from the dancer who grabbed the microphone.

"Thank you everyone. We are going to have a little break, so grab another drink, and then you'll get to meet our famous showgirl Violet Alegría, as well as our crowd favourite Rad Bad Fandango, and we have a new act for you that I think you'll all adore." The dancer bowed to the crowd's applause, then knelt down right in front of Elle, with her knees slightly apart, so Elle's gaze was level with her sequined g-string. Just when Elle thought she might die from wanting—yes, it was that dramatic—the dancer leaned forward and handed her an empty champagne glass.

"Meet me after the show at the bar and I'll get you a new one." The dancer projected her voice in a stage whisper and the crowd cheered.

"Do it, love." Some bloke's cheer made her grit her teeth. Elle really didn't want to be part of the show, but she also wanted to have a drink with the dancer, so she forced herself to nod and take the glass. Their fingers grazed each other, and a spiral of heat rushed across her skin. Hell.

The dancer stood up. "Thank you everyone. I'm The Gloved Gatsby." She bowed and walked off the stage.

Elle made it through the rest of the performance with a new appreciation for the show. Maybe it was feminist to own the stage like that and be in control of what people saw. Throughout the evening, Willow got drunker and sillier. Far out, what was Hugh thinking in marrying her? She was lovely, and of course, smoking hot, which had to be the attraction because he wasn't marrying her for her rational approach to life or her intelligence.

Elle sighed. When had she become so fucking judgemental? It'd been a disappointing year, and the year was only a few months old. Her boyfriend had dumped her the day before Christmas last year—in hindsight, she'd dodged a bullet there —and her job sucked. The daily drudgery meant she continually forgot that she had a plan. In another year, she would've saved up enough to launch her dream business. Yes, 2020 would be her year. She just needed to get through this year. Sticking it out in a boring job would be worth it in the end.

Maybe all she needed was some really good sex to restart some positivity in her life. She'd bang that dancer, that was for sure. As soon as the thought filled her head, Elle wanted to thump her forehead on the edge of the stage. It was one thing to crave the dancer's touch, and quite another to be so brutal in her wanting. But she could imagine the dancer bent slightly over the piano, with her long legs spread. Her fingers trembled as she thought about stroking them down the dancer's spine, leaving a red line in her skin with her fingernails, and listening to the dancer groan at her touch. If she wasn't surrounded by

Willow's drunk friends, she'd touch herself. Press her clit hard, as she slapped the dancer's bare arse. She could visualise the way her body would jerk forward from the slap, and the red palm mark on her arse. Elle wanted to kiss it better, then get on her knees behind the dancer and lick and suck at her until she screamed with pleasure.

"Elle. Are you alright?" Willow slung her arm around her.

"Ahh, yeah." She blinked, dragging herself out of her fantasy.

"We are going to grab a ride share car and head home now. The girls want to see my new place and Hugh told me not to stay out too late because we have plans tomorrow," Willow said.

"Okay. I might head home too." Elle hadn't forgotten about the plan to have lunch with her family and Willow's family. She didn't dread it; not really. Her family were big on appearances and while they'd been pleasantly cautious around her since she'd broken up with Campbell, she wasn't keen to be the single one at lunch with two families who were high on wedding nonsense. She stood up and gave Willow a quick hug. "See you tomorrow."

"This was so much fun." That high note entered Willow's voice again.

Elle smiled. "It was. I enjoyed it more than I thought I would." And if she had a drink, as promised, with the dancer afterwards, it might lead to more. Well, a girl could dream, anyway. She waited until Willow peeled herself out of their hug, then waved to all her friends as they picked up their purses and wandered out to the front. She sat alone for a few minutes. Normally, she'd pull out her phone and scroll her various social media apps, but she wasn't ready to escape from the cloud of lust around her just yet. Her imagination was more entertaining than anything the internet had to offer.

"Here is the replacement drink I promised." A flute of champagne appeared before her, and Elle turned her head towards the dancer's voice.

"Thanks. That was some trick." Oh God, she sounded so silly, or judgemental again. Didn't trick mean something else? Crap. That comment was certainly going on replay at three in the morning.

"Which one?"

Elle's throat was dry and she sipped the champagne. "Um, with the champagne down your leg."

The dancer grinned. "Awesome. I might have to keep it in my routine now that it's worked once."

"I was your first?" Elle wanted to slap her own forehead. How naïve did she sound?

The dancer laughed. "Yeah. Obviously I've practiced it a lot, but that was the first time I used it during a show."

A rush of heat flushed across her cheeks, and Elle wanted to shake her head to get rid of the heady sensation. She couldn't possibly be jealous of whoever had been the recipient of all those times the dancer had practiced it. Elle sipped her champagne again, except the dry tart notes of the champagne reminded her of the rush in her veins when the dancer had tipped champagne down her leg into Elle's mouth.

"My name is Charlie." The dancer held out her hand, and Elle shook it.

"Elle." Her skin burst into life at Charlie's touch. "I hate to ask this, but why me?" As soon as she asked the question, she wished she hadn't as Charlie gave her such a pointed look that she wanted to hide under the table.

"You looked so lonely in a group of happy people."

"Ouch." Although it was true; she didn't really belong with Willow's friends and had only gone because Hugh wanted them to be friends. Her own friends were more likely to go to a book club than giggle drunkenly at some dancers. Maybe she needed different friends? No. She liked talking about books, and she'd recently joined a class learning furniture restoration. It was run by an amazing trans woman, Sam, who was so welcoming with everyone. Elle was happy learning a skill that would help her business when she started it.

"Sorry."

"Don't be sorry. It's kind of true."

"Why go out with people if they aren't going to include you? I mean, Seraph's shows aren't cheap." Charlie sat in the chair next to her. She wore a red chiffon dressing gown wrapped around her slender dancer's frame, and the thin fabric didn't hide anything. Her tassel covered nipples were on display, as was the sequined g-string and stockings held up by suspenders. Fuck, she was so hot and so casually confident in her body.

"Willow is marrying my brother. He wanted me to go to her hen's night."

"Oh, family." There was some weight behind those two words, and Elle wanted to ask more.

"Yeah. Anyway, I enjoyed the show. I've never been to anything like this before, so I had no idea what to expect. You were really amazing." Elle stopped before she blurted out something about wanting to fuck her.

"So were you."

"What do you mean?"

"Not everyone in the audience is cool with getting involved, but you were great."

Elle flushed. "I even swallowed." Shit. "I mean, shit…"

Charlie roared with laughter. "Oh my God, that's hilarious." She clapped her hands and kept laughing until Elle had no option but to join in. Either that or actually hide under the table. "I'm sorry, but that's so funny."

"It's okay. I mean, I wasn't sure of the protocol."

Charlie was still giggling. "I'm pretty sure there isn't one, but you are so cool. Just going along with my nonsense."

No one had ever called her cool before—geeky, uptight, and bookish were words people usually wrongly used for her—so Elle just bit her lip and nodded. It was almost like Charlie could see through the carefully crafted façade. After a moment, Charlie reached up and brushed her thumb over Elle's lip.

"So pretty and cool with it. I bet you don't even know how beautiful you are with those dark brown eyes, staring at me like I'm special."

Elle swallowed. "What?"

"You have no idea, do you?" Charlie held Elle's chin between her thumb and forefinger and the heat from her touch spread across her face and down her throat.

"Um…"

"Can I kiss you?"

"Here?" Elle couldn't help glance around the room, still half full of people. To be fair, most of them stood near the bar in groups, and were paying her no attention at all. A few snuck glances at Charlie, and that was enough to remind her that she was in public. It was one thing to lust after someone—no one could see her thoughts—but another completely to kiss a stranger in public. A rush of heat burst along her spine. What would it be like?

Elle cleared her throat. "Yes, I would like that."

Charlie leaned forward in her chair and increased the pressure of her grip on Elle's chin. She brushed her lips gently against Elle's mouth, soft where she had expected bold and firm, and she almost moaned. It'd been so long since someone had cared for her like this; with a kiss that hinted at desire and lust, and she wanted it more than anything else.

"Come with me." Charlie dropped her hand away from Elle's face and stood up.

Elle slowly rose to her feet, a bit giddy with anticipation, and followed Charlie across the room. They threaded around the tables and chairs that filled the floor and went around the stage to a side door. Charlie opened it, and Elle walked through. As soon as the door closed, Charlie pushed Elle against the wall and kissed her. The loss of control would normally have Elle irritated, but for some reason, this was the hottest kiss she'd ever experienced. Had it been so long since she'd got laid that she'd willingly give up control? No, sex was the one part of her life where she didn't pretend she was meek.

She placed her hands on Charlie's shoulders—the dancer was quite a bit taller than her so she had to reach up—and purposely deepened the kiss. Charlie's rose perfume filled her nostrils, and she tasted like champagne with a touch of mint and something that must be purely Charlie. Charlie moaned and pressed her harder against the wall. Elle ground her hips against Charlie's thighs and willed her brain to figure out how to change this situation so she wasn't trapped. Her heart beat tripled in speed, and she kissed Charlie with a slow deliberation that communicated what she wanted.

Elle wanted to swap places with Charlie, to have her pressed against the wall, where she could control how she touched her gorgeous body. Every stroke of her tongue was strong—she might be smaller, but she determined their pace. Elle pushed Charlie's chiffon gown off her shoulders, and caressed down her sides, over her ribs, skirting the sides of her bare breasts.

"Touch me." Charlie's breath was raspy and frantic.

"Soon." Elle let her hands linger on Charlie's waist, before she spread her palms lower, over Charlie's lean arse. The round muscles were firm with the perfect softness; the combination of her dancer's strength and feminine curves was wonderful. Elle tilted her hips again, letting the fabric of her skirt slide over Charlie's long thighs, and still she kept kissing Charlie. Charlie kept her hands flat on the wall, beside Elle's head.

Yes. Elle wanted to command her to keep them there, but it'd been so long since she'd fucked someone that she didn't want to break their kiss. Instead, she sucked Charlie's tongue, then drifted her mouth down. Over her jaw, down her neck, and along her collar bone.

"The glue tastes pretty bad."

"Excuse me?" Elle lifted her head and stared up at Charlie.

"If you were thinking of removing the tassels and sucking my nipples, don't. The glue tastes pretty awful."

"Noted." Elle grabbed one of tassels and gave it a tug. Charlie gasped and it gave Elle the space she needed to push away from the wall and walked Charlie backwards, two steps to the wall on the other side of the hallway. Reluctantly, she shifted her grip off Charlie's fine arse, and held her hips, pushing gently until Charlie's breath huffed out with the soft impact of the wall. She gripped Charlie's hips tighter, slowly increasing the pressure to see how Charlie would respond. When she didn't flinch, even as Elle's fingers dug into her flesh, a fresh flush of heat raced down Elle's spine, collecting between her legs. She dropped to her knees, and slowly dragged her hands down Charlie's long legs, then back up again.

"Touch my hair," Elle said. She didn't wait for Charlie to respond. It was always such a negotiation the first time; working out each other's limits. She stroked her hands up Charlie's soft thighs, gently pushing them apart, although she was so lean from her dancing, there was enough of a gap for her hands to explore without needing her to step her feet apart.

With her thumbs, Elle traced along the edges of Charlie's g-string. The rough sequins contrasted with the softness of Charlie's skin, and the sensations grew as Charlie threaded her fingers through Elle's hair.

Yes. Elle leaned closer, kissing Charlie's thighs, slowly drifting her lips along until Charlie's fingers tightened on her scalp. Elle pushed Charlie's g-string aside, tilted her head and waited for a second.

"Please." Charlie's voice trembled. *So good.* Elle breathed in. Charlie's musky scent filled her nostrils and she licked. Taste exploded on her tongue. Oh fuck yeah, she'd really missed doing this. She licked and sucked and tasted, savouring all the flavours as she enjoyed the silky texture of Charlie's sex. Charlie moaned, loud in the echoey hallway, and her fingers gripped Elle's head tight. Elle knew Charlie was close, and she sucked on her clit hard. Over and over, and then she slowly sunk her fingers inside Charlie.

"So warm and tight," she whispered against her clit, then flicked it with her tongue, not giving Charlie any rest.

Charlie's breath was loud in the tight space of the hallway, and Elle adored the way the rhythm of her breathing matched the beat of Elle's heart and the pace of her fingers. She slid her fingers in and out of Charlie's vagina, continuing to work her clit with her tongue. The taste of her, so rich and delightful, was almost overwhelming, and Elle was close to coming herself. It would take more than this, but damn, it'd been so long, she could feel her body begging for someone's touch. She pushed her head harder against Charlie's mound, her tongue harder against her clit, and forced her fingers to move faster, until Charlie cried out, her inner muscles clenching around Elle's fingers.

Oh fuck yes. Elle kept up the pace until Charlie's fingers relaxed on her scalp, and then she staggered to her feet. Oof, she swayed, slightly faint in the head, and she leaned against Charlie.

"Fuck yeah. You are amazing," Charlie whispered against her, then slid her hands down Elle's sides. Elle pulled her skirt up, around her waist. "Touch me."

Charlie kissed her on the lips. "You taste wonderful too."

"Touch me." Elle needed her, and she grabbed Charlie's hands and moved them between her legs.

"So impatient." Charlie wasn't laughing, but there was a note of lazy humour in her voice. She slid her hands under Elle's lingerie and brushed over her clit.

Elle groaned.

"Yes, more of that."

Charlie didn't have to do much, the pressure of her fingers on Elle's clit was enough to send her spiralling over the edge.

She buried her face between Charlie's tits, tassels tickling her cheeks, and let the orgasm roll through her body. Fucking yes. Elle revelled in it; the delicious moment when her brain was quiet and her body thrilled. After a while, she lifted her head and Charlie kissed her on the forehead. Crap. The aftermath of these things was always awkward and Elle didn't give herself much time to recover before she straightened her skirt.

"Thanks." The urge to run away grew stronger.

"Want another drink?"

"I shouldn't."

Charlie laughed, that booming laugh that Elle had started to enjoy. "Yeah, neither should I, but when has good sense ever stopped me from anything?"

"Sure. Let's have a drink." Elle tried not to think too hard as she fiddled with the buttons on her shirt. It would always be a mystery to her that she could be so bold and commanding with sex and overthink every-fucking-other thing in her life.

1

POST-PANDEMIC. SUMMER.

The pandemic had been good to Elle. She cringed as the usual guilty flush spread over her skin whenever she thought that, but damn, it had been great for the interior decorating industry and especially her own business, D&Y Designs. It hadn't been that way at first; there was something wildly ridiculous about launching a new business a month before a global pandemic hit.

She'd spent most of February and March of 2020 panicking; except she need not have worried. With everyone stuck inside their homes constantly, they'd all wanted to finally fix their shitty bathrooms and upgrade or change their living rooms. People were tired of staring at the same thing all the fucking time, and she'd made a boat load of money helping people refurbish. Her business had expanded and now she employed two stylists, and a full-time accounts person. She was thinking of putting on two more people to help her cope with the workload, because they'd just won a huge tender for a mansion in Kensington. Doing an apartment for the daughter of media mogul Mr Inoue had opened so many doors and she didn't want to miss an opportunity because she didn't have the staff to cope. And she needed someone to look after the rental side of the business. Recently, she'd started dressing people's homes for sale, and had begun to collect items to use for creating beautiful photos. This side of the business was taking off too and she couldn't do everything.

There was only one thing lacking in her life. A partner to share her success with. Her parents had each other, and her brother Hugh had his wife, Willow, and their toddler, Joey, to keep them company. On the few moments when she wasn't run off her feet with work, she missed going out at night to book club or with her friends from her queer furniture making class. She missed them; between her new work and the pandemic, she hadn't been in contact with them for over a year.

She used to be a lot more social; like her fortnightly evening with Charlie at Seraph's Burlesque Club. For over a year, they'd had a glorious friends-with-benefits thing going on. It had been mostly just them fucking each other in all the different back stage rooms at Seraph's, and occasionally having a drink together. After a year, Elle still didn't know what Charlie did when she wasn't dancing, and she'd never talked about her plans to start her own business either. It was weird to think of Charlie now. How long had it been since she'd seen her? Too long. She pulled out her phone and quickly looked up Seraph's online. Oh, excellent, it had survived. And The Gloved Gatsby was dancing tonight.

"Fuck it. I deserve a night out." Elle rolled her eyes. She was talking to herself now? Hell. She clicked on the bookings tab and bought a ticket before she could second guess herself.

Elle paced out of the tube and pulled her mask off. Technically, they weren't compulsory anymore, but there was something about being on public transport with all those people that made her feel like she still needed the protection. Pandemic habits stuck hard. There was a bit of line outside the front of Seraph's, with various people chatting to each other in groups. Being here by herself was weird.

Everything was weird, even that thought, since she used to come here alone all the time. She didn't want anyone else getting in the way of her time with Charlie. She would come here to watch Charlie dance, have a drink and a chat with Charlie, and then have brilliant sex with Charlie. They'd never discussed being exclusive, and it hadn't mattered. Neither of them wanted a relationship; just a good fuck every now and then. The arrangement had suited them both. Elle swallowed. She'd changed and she wondered if she wanted to be exclusive with Charlie now, or if she simply wanted to say goodbye to that time in her life. Charlie had never given any indication she wanted something different to their arrangement. Did Charlie miss the casual easy way they just fit together? Maybe Elle should just go home before she made this weirder.

"Welcome to Seraph's. Can I see your ticket?" The Pacific Islander doorman was still the same, and some of the tension in her stomach eased. Some things hadn't changed. Elle pulled out her phone and opened the app with her ticket. He nodded.

Inside the room, nothing had changed, and it was a bit like stepping back into history. Slightly jarring because it was all so familiar, and yet time had touched it somehow too.

There were less tables, with more distance between them. Elle nodded to the white woman behind the bar.

"Hey. It's been an age. Charlie's friend, right?"

"Yes." Elle hadn't expected to be recognised but she'd been one of the regulars for a year, so it made sense even if it felt odd. "Please can I have a nip of whisky? On the rocks." She waved her phone over the pay device, then took the glass. She hadn't booked a table, never had since that first visit with Willow, and thankfully, she'd never seen Charlie do the champagne trick with anyone else. Huh! A pile of old memories threatened to overwhelm her and she gulped her whisky. The rich fluid burned her throat, getting rid of the bitterness on her tongue. It was illogical to be jealous of random people who might get the same dance move from Charlie as her. She leaned against the bar in her usual spot and waited.

Eventually the music lowered, and Charlie walked out on stage. She wore a spectacular blue dress that shimmered as she moved. A huge feathered headdress dominated Charlie's outfit and the stage. It must be bloody heavy, and yet, Charlie didn't seem to notice it. Her spine was tall and strong, and her limbs were just as lean as Elle remembered them.

Her fingers twitched against her glass. She took another sip, hoping that it would hide the faint tremor. Literally no one would notice except her; but she still wanted to cover it up. Damn it, she wasn't the person she'd been before the pandemic; desperate to have some fun while working a shitty boring job. Now she was a successful business owner. She'd been profiled in some of the UK's biggest interior design magazines, and she'd redesigned several homes for the rich and famous. She'd made it. Why did being here make her feel so irrelevant and small?

"Welcome to Seraph's Burlesque Club. I'm The Gloved Gatsby, and tonight we have an extraordinary collection of dancers and performers for you to enjoy."

Was it Elle's imagination, or did Charlie pause a little as she cast her view over the audience? Probably her imagination. The stage lights must make it impossible for Charlie to see her from up there.

"Grab a drink from the bar, and if you have seated tickets, your option of cheese board or dessert is on its way. Tonight we are raising money for the wonderful health care workers who got us through the pandemic. It was a rough time, and we pay our respects to everyone who died." Charlie bowed her head and a sombre silence fell over the club. After a moment, she lifted her head. "Make sure you round up your tab at the bar and we'll collate all the donations for the NHS Charities. Now, let's get into it. First up, we have one of Seraph's favourites: Violet Alegría."

The crowd applauded and the curtains drew back. A 1960s Mini sat on the stage; a whole fucking car, and Elle put her drink down to clap along with the rest of the astonished crowd. She'd been backstage here often enough with Charlie. How the hell did they get a car up there? The music started up, and the door of the car opened. Out stepped a beautiful woman in a bright red 1950s dress that billowed out from her hips. She leaned against the car, posing like a model in an old magazine, and slowly began to dance.

"Hey. I thought it was you." Charlie's whisper was hot against her ear.

Elle turned slowly. "Hi." Her pulse sped up as she tilted her face towards Charlie, who had taken off the giant feathered headdress. The height of her heels made her even taller than usual, so Elle had to look up towards her.

"I wasn't sure if you'd ever come back."

She shouldn't have stayed away for so long because the familiar warmth from Charlie's body settled the riot in her belly. So much had happened since they'd last seen each other; would it be possible to carry on where they'd left off? Elle wanted so much more now. More than a quick fuck and a laugh; more than just the highlight of her crappy week. She had her dream business now and it made her greedy enough to want more in the rest of her life too. Maybe Charlie wouldn't be the right person. Or maybe she would. They'd been friends with benefits on a shallow level. Would they connect on a deeper plane? Or would this be one final fuck before Elle moved on?

"Is this weird?" Elle tried to sum it all up with a whisper as Violet Alegría pulled off her glove with her teeth and cast it aside. The kitty ducked into the light for a second to pick it up.

"Is that Reiko Inoue?"

Surely not, Elle must be seeing things. Why on earth would one of her wealthiest clients work here?

"Yes. She works here."

"But…" Elle clamped her mouth shut. It was none of her business where someone chose to work. Reiko certainly didn't need the money. "Never mind, it's not my business."

"How do you know our Reiko?"

"I—" Shit. What could she say? What if Reiko hadn't told anyone here about her life outside of Seraph's? "Through work."

"Are you at the university?" Charlie leaned closer, close

enough for Elle to feel the warmth of her body, even if they weren't quite touching. She tried to suppress the shiver that traversed her skin.

"No. I'm an interior designer."

Charlie grinned. "Seriously? How did I not know that?"

Elle choked. "Um, we didn't really spend much time talking, you know… before."

The bark of Charlie's laugh made Elle glow. Fuck, she'd missed that. Being able to make Charlie laugh was one of the things that had kept Elle going when her job was a drudge and her plan to start her own business seemed so far away.

"I'm glad you came back." Charlie kissed her on the cheek, then disappeared.

Elle watched her as she disappeared behind the bar, careful not to pull the crowd's attention away from the dancer on stage. Violet Alegría had dropped the dress onto the bonnet of the Mini, and was dancing to Elvis' Jailhouse Rock in her corset and g-string. With a start, Elle realised that the dancer was her client, Yolande, Reiko's partner. When they'd hired her to work on their new apartment, she hadn't made the connection, but thinking back over her time at Seraph's, she'd never seen Violet Alegría dance, so it wasn't a connection she ought to have made. She was glad because it might have been weird doing their décor if she'd known. Even now, sitting here watching, her heart galloped at the idea that her worlds were colliding.

She'd always assumed that her time at Seraph's was her own personal special place that no one in the rest of her life knew about. Willow had never mentioned her hen's night again, something Elle was thankful for, because she knew she'd blush and that would open up all manner of questions. That first time with Charlie had been exactly what she'd needed to give her hope for a better future. And look at her now. Pride settled over her; she'd come a long way since Willow's hen's night. She'd created the life she'd wanted, and yes, some of that was thanks to Charlie. She ought to thank her for being the positive moments she'd needed. No, she couldn't say that without it being awkward.

Violet Alegría—Yolande—bowed to the audience who clapped and whistled their appreciation, and then just as the curtains began to close, Charlie walked out on stage. She'd put her headdress back on. Warmth filled Elle's torso with a little prickle of hot anticipation, as Charlie smiled at the audience.

"Let's give another big thank you to Violet Alegría. Isn't she wonderful?" Charlie strutted back and forth in front of the curtains, each stride emphasising her long legs under her sparkly blue dress. "Who wants to see a bit of this?" Charlie slid her dress up her thigh, and the room filled with noise. Elle raised up her glass and grinned.

"Tonight's dance is for someone special. For a good friend of mine who loves champagne." Charlie dipped her head with an exaggerated wink in her direction and Elle tried not to hide.

Surely the audience wouldn't stare at her, she was one of several people leaning on the bar, so Charlie could be referring to anyone in her vicinity. The music changed, flowing effortlessly into Quavo's Champagne Rose, and Charlie began to dance, rolling her hips to the slow hip hop beats. Elle stopped caring who was looking at her because she only had eyes for Charlie. Charlie, who taunted her by tracing her gloved hand down her leg, in the same path as the champagne had flowed that first night years ago. She stood on one leg, holding her other out in front of her, and reached down to touch her toes. A flash of bright red nail polish caught the light above, and Elle gulped. Charlie wore impossibly high open toed stilettos, and the shoes had a fragile look with thin blue straps holding them to Charlie's feet. How she could balance on one of them was a mystery to Elle.

Elle had learned early in life to embrace her geeky side. She'd always been the last to be selected for any type of sport at school and she didn't blame anyone for that. Being able to catch a ball wasn't something she'd ever excelled at, and her balance wasn't great either. A warm admiration filled her chest as she watched Charlie move her body with elegance and a certain free spirit that Elle would never have. Knowing that Charlie willingly shared her glorious body with Elle made it even better.

Could they pick up where they'd left off?

2

Charlie winked at the audience. It'd been months since they'd opened the doors of Seraph's to the public again and she loved being up here—mostly. She plastered a wide grin on her face and bounced from hip hop into an old school Charleston as the music changed on cue. Burlesque was her dream job. Ever since she'd discovered it as a teenager, it'd been all she'd ever wanted to do. And she'd done it successfully for years before the fucking pandemic changed everything. She almost missed the next step in her routine, wobbling slightly on her heels, before she shoved that thought away where it belonged. Discarded forever, like the shitty time it'd been. Charlie was a performer—born and bred—having been on stage and film since before she could walk. This was her dream job.

She refused to let her smile slip as she went through the motions of her routine. When she pulled the huge feathers from her head and used them as a fan, she tried not to ponder why the applause from the audience didn't hit the same way as it used to. Charlie lifted her chin, keeping her spine straight and shook her tits. She was too much of a professional performer to let anyone know her feelings. When she undid her bra and used her fans to tease the audience before they got the final glimpse of her fucking incredible fit body, she waited for the crowd to cheer her. The noise always filled her with joy. One last shimmy and a bow, then she let the curtain fall in front of her. Her grin slipped and she sucked in a deep breath. Shit, maybe she wasn't as fit as she thought she was. She had worked bloody hard on regaining her fitness and still her chest pounded as she walked off stage. She had precisely fifteen seconds to compose herself before the curtain opened again and she needed to introduce Dan and his hula hoop act.

Charlie put the feathered fans on a chair and peeked through the curtains. It wasn't really the done thing, but she really needed to get some energy from this crowd.

"Hello everyone." Charlie stepped through the curtain and Ben opened them up. "Wasn't that dancer just wonderful?" The crowd laughed. "I know, I know. I'm pretty great. Before I introduce our next dancer, make sure you donate to the NHS Charities before you leave tonight." She paused and gestured to the bar, loving the way a bunch of the audience sheepishly turned to the bar, then spun in their chairs to stare at her again.

"Tell me. What's the hardest thing about joining the circus?" Charlie didn't wait for an answer. "They make you jump through all sorts of hoops first." A few people chuckled. "Yeah, I know, it's not the best hula hoop joke. Maybe you have to be in the right social circle to get it." More people laughed and she bowed. "Hands up who learned a new hobby during the fucking lockdowns?"

"Fucking useless government." Someone in the audience

jeered; there was always some loud mouth. He had a point. Obviously the lockdowns sucked, but opening up too soon had only resulted in more harm. She'd rather think about new hobbies; like Dan and his hula hoops.

"Anyone? No? Our next act thought about running away to the circus when he was a kid, but it wasn't until the lockdown happened that he finally decided to pick up a few tricks. Please welcome Dan Dan the Hoop Man to the stage." She stepped to the side of the stage and waved her hand. Dan walked onto stage wearing his signature Union Jack sparkly hot pants. He didn't bother with a shirt, only wearing suspenders clipped to his hot pants.

"Aren't his boots amazing? I wish I could balance on heels that high." Charlie waggled her own foot to the audience and a few people laughed. "Anyway, to Dan! Give him and his hoops a huge cheer."

"One hoop. What kind of crappy show is this?" The man stood up and then yelled a slur at Dan.

Charlie sneered at him. "None of that, mister. Seraph's is an inclusive show."

"Jealousy just spurs us on to greater things." Dan circled his sole hoop on his arm in the most basic of tricks, while Walter escorted the man from the floor. Most of the audience clapped in support of his removal. Once he was gone, Charlie traced her hand down her side and slapped her own hip.

"Speaking of greater things, who is ready for some hula hoop action?" The crowd cheered and she let the glow fill up her happiness well again. Yes, this really was her dream job. Ben, their IT specialist and stage technician, changed the music to Dan's chosen tune and she walked backwards off the stage to watch from the wings. Dan began with only one hoop, twisting his body through the hoop as it spun around his limbs, then his waist. Slowly he picked up another hoop, then another, until he was spinning several hoops along his arms and around his waist. Charlie grinned as he did her favourite trick; spinning hoops at different speeds to create an incredible optical illusion. The spontaneous applause from the crowd was great; Dan deserved every accolade for this act. Even though she'd seen it once a week for the last six months, it was still amazing to her that he'd never touched a hula hoop before… before.

After a couple more acts, Charlie got an update on their charitable donations for the evening and when she announced the figure, the crowd's applause was the loudest of the night.

"Come on, you can all do more. If you have enough money to come out and enjoy everything Seraph's has to offer, you can spare a bit more change for those who need it." It was this part of the night that she loved the most, when the audience was a bit tipsy and they started to lose their inhibitions and interact with the performers. She always saved up the new performers for this part of the evening because they were guaranteed to get a positive reaction from the crowd and that would give them confidence for the next time they got up on stage.

A couple of hours later, the audience started to filter out and go home, and she'd avoided talking to Elle for long enough. Why did part of her hope that she'd already left? They'd always been good together, one of Charlie's favourite hook ups, but as much as she didn't want to admit it to herself, she'd changed since then.

"You were fantastic." Elle's praise fell flat; much like everything since before. What was wrong with her?

"Thanks."

Elle brushed her finger between Charlie's eyebrows. "What's wrong?"

"Nothing." Charlie schooled her features into a neutral expression. All those years of acting classes were worth it for moments like this when she wasn't ready to discuss feelings with a hook up. They'd never had that type of relationship, and Charlie wasn't keen to figure out if Elle wanted the same or something different.

"Sure."

"It's nothing much. I just feel a bit off."

"Are you getting sick?" Elle asked and Charlie shook her head.

"Fuck no. No."

"Okay. Sorry."

Charlie cleared her throat and Elle gave her such a side-eyed glance, that she couldn't help but laugh. That's why Elle was one of her favourite hook ups; because she always made her laugh even when she didn't much feel like it. "Want a drink?"

"I shouldn't, but someone I know once said that unwise decisions often resulted in fun, so yeah, I'll have a drink."

The familiar glow that Charlie usually got from an adoring audience came now, as Elle quoted her back to herself. "Ha. Funny."

Elle walked towards the bar, leaving Charlie to catch up. She wrapped her thin overcoat around her, suddenly wishing that she'd thrown on something more than the chiffon coat before embarking on her usual chit chat with the crowd who lingered for another drink or two after the show. Elle leaned forward on the bar and her skirt pulled tight across her round backside. She hadn't changed much since Charlie had last seen her; still had the same perfectly plump arse and soft limbs. Her rounded stomach and hips filled Charlie's hands whenever she was lucky enough to touch her. Charlie was tempted to rest her hand on Elle's arse, but she refrained.

It was Charlie who had changed; this uncertainty wasn't fun and not something she wanted to dwell on. She used to have brash confidence, able to stand tall in front of anyone and state her piece without doubt. Had she always been so shallow that she hadn't needed to suffer anxiety? She wanted to rub her throat. She'd been happy before all that stuff had happened, and she'd assumed she'd go right back to being happy again. Why hadn't she? What was wrong with her? Nothing. Nothing at all. Fuck it.

Elle laughed at something Reiko said. "I'm so glad Captain is starting to enjoy his space."

"Captain?" Charlie wanted her old buzz back. If she had to force it, then she would.

"Our cat. Elle designed an amazing indoor play space for Captain and Bounce." Reiko smiled as she passed Elle a flute of champagne.

"I thought you said you did interior design?"

Elle turned slightly, and the light above the bar shone on her black hair. "I do."

Charlie's fingers twitched, wanting to stroke Elle's hair, to feel the smooth strands under her palms, and hopefully wrap it around her fist and pull, just like Elle liked. She blinked to focus on the conversation, not things she couldn't have.

"For cats?"

Elle laughed. "For people as well, but yes, we do include

people's pets in their custom designs. Pets are family members. Their needs should be included in any functional design."

"You really are a designer."

Reiko clicked her tongue. "Charlie. Be nice to the guests."

"Oh, it's okay. Elle is my friend."

"All the more reason to be kind to her."

Charlie raked her gaze over Elle with purpose. "I think my kindness isn't in doubt."

"Charlie." Elle's warning note only gave Charlie more bravado.

"I'm surprised Reiko didn't recognise you from all your past visits to Seraphs. I guess she only expects me to be kind to all our guests and doesn't expect the same from you?" Charlie didn't mean to sound as snarky as that came out. She hated being off balance like this. Why couldn't her life be simple, like it used to be?

"Careful, Charlie. Not everyone's job requires them to interact with our guests."

"I'm right here," Elle jumped back into the conversation. "Anyway, I'm pleased that grumpy Captain is happy with the arrangement we made for him."

"So am I. I was really worried that he wouldn't be able to climb up."

Charlie tapped her toe against the edge of the bar. "Heaven forbid if the cat couldn't climb."

"Charlie." Elle glared at her and she deserved it. She was being a bitch. Why couldn't she stop?

"Yeah, fine. Yah for the cat. I'll see you guys tomorrow." Charlie spun on her heels and marched towards the stage door. She needed to be by herself, rub one out alone, or something. Anything to get rid of this frustration that beat a drum against her chest. Burlesque was her dream job, but ever since they'd opened Seraph's again, each night had left her empty and unsatisfied. It pissed her off, rather royally, because she'd spent the whole fucking pandemic aching to be back on stage with people cheering for her. She'd craved the energy of a show and had ignored all the medical advice to stay home and isolate because she needed an audience; until it was too late.

"Charlie. What's the matter?" Elle must have followed her across the room and Charlie turned to glare at her. She didn't need anyone else. Certainly, she didn't need anyone to see her now as she struggled for air.

"Nothing." Her breath was short again. Fucking COVID. The vaccine had helped ease her long term symptoms but she still had to fight for breath sometimes and she hated it.

"I don't believe you." Elle persisted and Charlie increased her glare, trying to bore holes in her skin with her expression. The soft expression in Elle's dark brown eyes stole all her energy and her frustration softened.

"It's complicated." Too complex to talk about with someone she used to hook up with. "Shall we fuck?" At least she could expend some of this rioting nonsense with an orgasm.

Elle tilted her head, considering. "I'm not sure."

"Fine. I'll find someone else." Charlie stormed through the stage door with her head held high. She sure as fuck didn't understand what was happening to her, and she wasn't about to show Elle any uncertainty. Elle had always known how to push her sexually, always in control when Charlie wanted to get lost in sensation. If there was anyone who would lose all respect for Charlie if she showed any doubts, it was Elle. Strong, sexy, confident Elle who adored Charlie's stage persona and only wanted to fuck The Gloved Gatsby. There was nothing real between them.

Charlie sighed. If only she could keep pretending that all she wanted was the shallow performance that had been her whole life before. Before she had to spend a whole fucking year inside, trying to deal with an online version of work, with no human interaction apart from her housemates. And when she'd gotten sick, they'd moved out, leaving her alone. All she wanted was her old life back again. She didn't appreciate having to figure out how to get back to the past—where she'd been happy—while sorting through all this new stuff that had been part of her life recently.

3

_____

Charlie snuck in the back door of Seraph's the next afternoon. Yes, she was avoiding everyone, especially Beth who was bound to quiz her about last night's nonsense with Elle and Reiko. Everyone knew the fundamental rule of burlesque. Always be good to the kitty. She was the worst type of dancer to take out her frustration on the person whose sole task was to help her. The kitty wasn't just any staff member, she was the key that held the whole show together. Charlie had been doing burlesque for long enough that she ought to be able to deal with her own crap without it impacting on her colleagues.

Once she'd dumped her stuff in her locker in the office she shared with Beth, she'd compose herself and then apologise. First to Reiko, and then to Beth for generally upsetting the balance between everyone. Beth believed that the core team at Seraph's were her family. Did that make Beth the mother of them all? She certainly mothered their emotional needs; hence why Charlie wasn't that keen to admit anything at all to her. Beth would see through her façade to the drama underneath.

And Charlie was not ready to confront that mess yet. Maybe never.

"Hello." Elle stood in the hallway beside Beth, both of them between the back door and Charlie's office. Having an office space was one of the benefits of being the MC at Seraph's. She had her own desk and computer where she planned the schedule for every evening, organised the dancers, and helped with planning the dance classes too. Elle was here? And not just here, but inconveniently in her way. Charlie's spine stiffened. Who had she pissed off to give her this crap in her life?

"What are you doing here?"

"Charlie." Beth's warning rushed right past her, like a flashing sign that she deliberately ignored. What was Elle doing here with Beth? Had she come to find out why Charlie had rejected her last night? That'd never bothered her before. If she'd come here to get some sort of apology from Charlie…

Charlie refused to sigh in front of Elle and Beth. The weakness inside her was no one else's business, and she'd bloody well fix it herself. Stubbornness was a strength that she valued in herself. That, and independence and an ability to solve her own problems. Growing up on different television sets had instilled those qualities in her.

"Reiko recommended me to Beth for the redesign."

"We are doing a redesign? Since when?"

Beth frowned in her direction. "You might be the MC, Charlie, but this is my business and I'll run it how I like."

"Of course." With some effort, Charlie ducked her gaze low. She had enough good sense not to spit on the hand that provided her dream job—dream, ha, that coated her tongue in a bitter flavour, as if she'd just bitten into a bad apple. All pretty on the outside and floury, bitter, and rotten on the inside. "What do you need from me?"

"Nothing at this stage." Beth dismissed her with a glance that left the rest unsaid—that Beth had plenty to say to her once they were alone.

"Okay. Hi Elle. Good luck." Charlie brushed past them, down the hallway, and threw her bag into her locker. In an hour, she had a class with some beginner burlesque dancers, and after that, a woman had booked a photography session.

During the pandemic, they'd had a massive uptick in random people who wanted to dress up in burlesque outfits and have professional photos taken. It'd been an accidental bonus for the business. Their old stage technician, Arya, had moved home with her parents when the first lockdown hit and Beth hadn't planned to replace Arya because there was no need for a stage tech when they couldn't open to the public.

One afternoon, Beth had arrived with Ben at her side. She'd met him online and employed him as their new tech. Typical Beth, and she still hadn't mentioned what they were doing online when they met. Ben had instantly proved he had a superior ability with all things technical and was a brilliant photographer to boot. He didn't speak much, preferring to stay out of the limelight. It'd been his idea to offer the public photo shoots in all the brilliant costumes Ace created. Reiko and Steph helped dress the stage, Ben created incredible lighting, and Charlie did the person's outfit, makeup, hair, and poses. It was a great side-earner.

Charlie marched down to the costume room and started to compile the outfits that today's client, Sarah, had chosen from their online catalogue. Hopefully she hadn't given them the wrong sizes, which was something that happened far too often.

Ben had set up their website so people selected their size, and then they were able to pick outfits for their photo shoot based on that. If they underestimated their size, they'd end up with the wrong list and it always wasted everyone's time.

Charlie turned on her computer. It was time to do some cynical cyber stalking so she could guess Sarah's size and bring a few alternatives, just in case.

"Why do you have a stick up your arse?" Beth didn't mince any words as she leaned on the doorway.

"Nothing."

"Bullshit."

"Fine. It's something but I don't want to talk about it."

Beth nodded. The wonderful thing about Beth was that she accepted Charlie's crap and knew when to leave something alone.

"Something to do with work or something else?" Unless it impacted on Seraph's, of course.

"Everything." Charlie sighed. She should have known Beth would want more of an explanation, especially since she'd included Seraph's in her vague explanation. Well, it was the truth. Everything was the fucking problem and that was why it was a problem. She used to be happy, living her best life, and now it just didn't give her the same satisfaction.

"Tell me." Beth had the whole mother hen vibe happening, and Charlie breathed out slowly. If she didn't say anything, Beth wouldn't give up until she did. There were only a couple of people in Charlie's life who were more stubborn than herself, and Beth was one of them.

"I don't know what to say. I don't even understand it myself. I was so desperate to get back on stage after… and now I'm here and it feels off." Charlie still enjoyed dancing, she still loved interacting with the audience, she loved the attention, but it just didn't give her the same high that she used to get. She missed the way dancing used to make her feel. Her life used to be carefree.

"I think the whole thing affected everyone more than any of us want to admit," Beth spoke slowly, quietly, and Charlie bit back the urge to push away the kind comment.

"Yeah. Something like that."

"I haven't seen it affecting your work yet, so don't stress too much. I'm here if you want to talk about it, whenever you are ready."

"Thanks. Sorry about grumping at Elle."

Beth nodded. "I didn't realise you knew Elle, and I don't know what happened between you and Elle. It's obvious there is some kind of history there." Beth held up her hand. "You don't have to tell me. All I want is for you to try and get past whatever the issue is and get along with her. She's going to be spending a bit of time here over the next few weeks."

If it wasn't such a big deal, Charlie would've scoffed at Beth. Beth likely wanted to know everything and was only exercising patience because she needed to. Despite the urge to breathe in and out loudly, Charlie swallowed.

"No problem. I shouldn't have taken out my frustrations on her."

"Or anyone."

"Yeah." She couldn't find the energy for a snarky come-back. "Soon. I'll do it soon."

"Thanks. And hey, Charlie?"

"Yeah?"

"You can talk to me anytime. You are an important part of Seraph's, and your wellbeing matters to me."

Beth left before Charlie could snarl at her. Sure, if that was true, where was Beth when Charlie was in hospital with COVID?

Charlie coughed. She'd been so oblivious back in March 2020, ignoring all the advice. The last thing she wanted to do was stop going to work; and when Seraph's had closed, she'd been so angry at Beth. People said COVID was just like the flu. What was the big deal? Why close up shop? Charlie had picked up work at a few underground clubs, still dancing, still loving the attention, still getting paid. And it'd kept her happy for a while, until she'd caught the bloody sickness and ended up in hospital.

It wasn't just the flu. If she hadn't been so sick, she would've been angry at the people who'd misled her, but ultimately, the person she was most annoyed with was herself. She hadn't wanted to stop working, hadn't wanted to be stuck in her house, locked down away from the people who fuelled her and gave her energy. Her defiance had led to her illness. It was her own fault and she growled under her breath; she'd rather be mad than face the truth and forgive herself. Neither option was going to resolve her current problem with enjoying her work.

"Are you okay?" Elle asked. Fucking hell, was everyone going ask the same question? Charlie dropped her hands to her lap.

"Of course."

"You were holding your throat."

Charlie shook her head. "It's nothing." When she'd been in hospital, they'd put a ventilator pipe down her throat to help her breathe. Even though so much time had passed since then, her throat still remembered, like a phantom scar or something weird.

"Okay. I just wanted to ask if you are okay with me potentially working here for a while."

"Sure. Why wouldn't I be?"

"I just wanted to check, that's all."

Charlie shrugged. "It's fine."

Elle frowned. "You don't sound like it's fine."

"Oh, for fuck's sake." Charlie flung out her arms. "Damn it. Look, not everything is about you."

Elle grimaced, then nodded. "Sure. Well, I won't be around too much. I'm just putting together a plan and some costs, and then I'll just deal with Beth until she confirms what she wants done. I'll have to oversee contractors, but if you want me to give you some space, that should be easy enough."

"Elle. I don't want space from you." Charlie didn't know what she wanted. Being pushed away by Elle wasn't any kind of solution to her current malaise. She liked people, she wanted to go back to her old life, where she danced and people cheered for her, and she had a whole group of different hook ups. It'd been fun. The best sort of fun.

"You don't?"

"No."

Elle shrugged and held up her palms. "Okay. I don't know what's going on, and I guess that's okay. I mean, we haven't seen each other in ages. People change and we didn't have a close friendship anyway." Elle nailed the problem; people changed, even Charlie, not that she wanted to think too hard about how she'd changed.

"We didn't." Charlie didn't want to notice the way Elle

half-turned and began to walk away with a dejected expression. "What we did have was fun. Elle…" She gulped.

"Yeah?" Elle turned back towards Charlie, who couldn't help but feel warm at the sight of her open expression.

"Yes. I don't want to ruin that just because I'm having a shit time at the moment. Kiss me better?"

Elle chuckled. "If I thought it would help, then I'd leap at the chance."

"Why wouldn't it help?"

"Just a feeling I have."

Charlie rubbed her forehead. "Am I so obvious?" She barely understood herself; how could anyone else see what the fuck was happening to her?

"Yes and no." Elle waggled her head side to side.

"What does that mean?"

Elle grinned. "Relax. Maybe it's just my memory playing a trick on me."

"Oh?"

"I remember you as this confident dancer who deserved all the attention the crowd threw your way. I don't recall you ever showing this—"

"Doubt." Charlie didn't wait for Elle to say it. She spoke over the top of Elle, filling the space with the truth.

"I was going to say uncertainty."

"Isn't that the same thing?"

Elle leaned against the door. "I guess so. Doubt is a bit stronger than uncertainty. Everyone has uncertainty, not everyone doubts themselves. What happened to you?"

"Why did something have to happen?"

Elle's eyebrows raised up. "Did you not notice the whole pandemic and lockdowns and stuff?"

The urge to tell Elle to fuck off rose in Charlie's throat like a boiling hot ball of lava. "Obviously." She rolled her eyes instead.

"Something like that is going to have an impact on people. On me and on you, on everyone. I think it's probably natural to notice some changes in the way you approach the world after going through something as difficult as all of that." Elle waved her hand. It was odd how no one really wanted to name it, like it'd been so hard and overwhelming that just the name —COVID, coronavirus, the rona, Delta strain, whatever— jabbed people with a painful memory. Charlie shrugged.

"If you want to talk about it, I'm here." Elle paused for a bit. "I mean, I know we didn't really have that type of thing going on…"

"Thanks." Charlie almost left it there but something in Elle's expression eased the churning in her gut. "Um, there is one thing I don't get."

"Yeah?"

"Why now? I didn't have any doubts during the whole fucking thing. I mean, I hated the lockdown and trying to run shows and dance classes using online programs just sucked, but this…"

"Feeling?"

"Yeah, that. It didn't start until after everything was, well, I don't want to say back to normal, but you know, mostly sorted." The whole mess was so complicated; because not every country had access to vaccines as fast as they had in the UK and that meant each country had very different experiences. Charlie had plenty of friends who had relatives in other countries. London had always been a global city with connections everywhere.

Elle chewed her bottom lip. "I read a bit about this recently. There's a theory that it's impossible to process something traumatic while experiencing it, and it's not until afterwards, once your body is safe, that your mind kind of catches up and can focus on healing."

"Well, that's annoying."

Elle laughed, a quiet gentle laugh that wrapped around Charlie like a soft blanket. "I agree."

"Can I just refuse to deal with this forever?"

Elle tipped her head back and her laugh boomed around the room. Damn it, Charlie used to laugh like that before. "You can make any decision you want. But tell me this. Will burying these feelings fix them?"

"No." Charlie hated the way she sounded like a sullen toddler.

"Then you probably need to figure it out sometime."

"Fuck you." Charlie laughed and shook her head. "Fine. But I don't like it."

Elle bit her lip again and Charlie wanted to know what she wasn't saying. Or maybe she didn't want to know.

"Tell me about this redesign Beth has planned." Charlie needed to talk about something else, and from the way Elle's eyes lit up and her lips stretched into a smile, maybe she felt the same way.

"Given the budget, it'll be a light touch in terms of what we can actually change. Beth wants to see if we can change some of the functionality behind the public areas, so if you aren't bothered by me working here, then it'd be great to get your opinions on what could be changed."

Charlie grinned. "Oh my god, can we finally change the

fucking hallway onto the stage? It's so narrow and impossible to get some of the costumes up there easily."

"I was incredibly impressed with the car on stage last night."

"Yeah, we had to put in a special ramp for it, but it means we've lost a whole dressing room. Worth it though." Charlie was pretty proud of the way they'd found a solution to that one. Yolande's new dance with the car looked incredible.

"Let's go and have a look." Elle pushed herself off the doorframe and left the room, and Charlie followed her. She liked following Elle and her pulse skipped a beat.

4

————

For Elle to focus on work just after Charlie's admission took some doing. When they'd hooked up after a show, they'd chatted and had a fun friendship. This was different; it was deeper with the way that Charlie spoke about her doubts. For the whole time they'd hooked up, Elle had never mentioned her job and they'd only talked about the show that evening, laughing about the audience, or simply rushing back-stage to fuck before Elle collapsed in a ride share and went home to sleep. It'd worked simply because being with Charlie was her escape from that part of her life, and she'd never given any thought to how it affected Charlie.

This was her job, her life, and Elle had walked in and out of it without much care. All she'd seen was Charlie's confidence and she'd assumed her life had no problems. Oh, that was why this didn't hit right, because she ought to have known. Had she been so absorbed by her own issues that she hadn't noticed Charlie properly? No one had a perfect life. The idea that Charlie might have worries and doubts as much as

Elle did shouldn't have been this much of a surprise. How much had Elle gained from surrounding herself with Charlie's confidence?

"This way." Charlie opened a door in the rabbit warren of hallways and doors in the back stage area at Seraph's and indicated for Elle to follow her. Elle had, typically, marched off without knowing where she was going. Charlie wore tight blue jeans—tight enough to be almost painted on her long dancer's legs—and they left nothing to the imagination, with every step drawing Elle's attention to Charlie's arse, hips, and waist. A loose sleeveless shirt hung down her spine with Charlie's strong arms swinging beside her. She moved with efficiency, smooth and supple. Elle's fingers twitched with the need to touch Charlie, to skim her hands down Charlie's straight spine, and across the curves of her hips.

Elle had some knowledge of the place, given that Charlie had often dragged her back here into different spaces so they could fuck, but she really needed a plan so she could redesign it all to be more functional. These old buildings always ended up like this, with little changes and additions over the years until the whole space made little sense. Beth had taken advantage of a newly announced government grant to assist creative arts spaces in reopening to the public, and the grant could provide a lot of improvements to Seraph's if Elle planned carefully.

"Walk me through something." It was time to stop salivating over Charlie's body and start thinking about work. She was here to do a job for Beth. Hanging out with Charlie was a bonus, a side benefit, and she shouldn't be so distracted by her.

Charlie spun around. "What?"

"When we get to the stage, I want you to walk me through your routine in the evening."

Charlie frowned. "From the stage? Or from the beginning?"

"The beginning would be better, actually. Can we do that? Do you have time?" Elle shouldn't assume that Charlie could drop all her other work to help her.

"I have…" Charlie checked her phone. "…about half an hour before I have a dance class to run."

"Where do you hold those?"

"We have a warm up room next to the stage—you've been in there before—" Charlie winked, "—and sometimes I get the class up on the stage so they can perform what they've been learning."

"Okay." Elle paused, finding it impossible to ignore the memory of Charlie with her hands tied to the barre in the warm up room. She'd used a long silk rope to tie Charlie up before she'd washed off her makeup and her glue. Burlesque glue wasn't very tasty, and there was something sensual about being the person to clean Charlie after her show; to be the one who exposed her nipples to the air, then sucked them until Charlie begged to have her hands released. Elle shivered. *Work, think about work.*

"Um, what other events do you hold?" Elle had assumed Seraph's Burlesque Club was only open at night for live events, but the idea that they held dance classes during the day opened up a lot more possibilities for how people used the space. She'd need to understand it all before she planned any changes.

Charlie raised one eyebrow. "You can get the schedule from Beth."

"I know. But I like talking to you." Elle pinched her lips together. Shit. She shouldn't have admitted that—not when she was attempting to stay focused on her job—but Charlie just grinned, then winked.

"It's because I have nice tits, isn't it?"

Elle's face bloomed with heat and she stammered, unable to get out a functional word.

"Ha, look at you. I shouldn't tease, but it's such fun." Charlie bumped Elle's elbow with her hand and barked out her big laugh. "Okay. So we obviously have the evening events with different shows. We do burlesque shows from Thursday to Sunday. We are shut on Monday nights, and on Tuesday and Wednesday we have a couple of other things, like drag trivia and sometimes a band or other live music. Mostly, Seraph's is a typical bar with live entertainment. We hold dance classes during the day for people who want to learn burlesque, and thanks to Ben, the tech, we also do photography sessions for people who want a professional photo of themselves in a burlesque costume but don't want to actually perform."

"That's a thing?" Elle had so much to learn about this business before she began the redesign of their spaces.

"Yeah. Funny, isn't it? A lot of our clients are women who want a pretty photo of themselves to give as a gift to their partner, and a burlesque costume shows off a lot of skin in an elegant way without being totally nude. It's really popular. We get a few men too, mostly thanks to Ace and Jack's connections."

"Okay, and where do you do that?"

"We usually take the photos on the stage. The lighting is

the best, and people like to have the framing of the stage curtains and unfocused sense of audience."

Elle couldn't imagine wanting to give someone an almost nude photo of themselves, but then, people sent naked selfies all the time. Just because she wouldn't do it didn't really mean anything, and she'd have loved to have a photo of Charlie that had been created just for her. A rough lump filled her throat and she swallowed. *Focus on work.*

"Okay, so you need quite a versatile space with room for different types of uses, as well as enough planning to ensure it can be potentially used in ways that you aren't doing now."

"Sure."

"Do you disagree?" Elle heard an odd note in the tone used by Charlie. Had she missed something?

"No. That all sounds good, but I don't understand how Beth can afford this. I mean, we've been doing really well since stuff reopened—"

It wasn't Elle's place to talk about the grant that Beth had acquired for Seraph's. "That's a conversation you'll have to have with her. It's not really my place to discuss my client's budget without permission."

"Not even for me?" Charlie had a quizzical expression and Elle frowned. "It's fine. Don't tell me. I'm teasing."

"Okay." Elle tried to relax. They used to tease each other like this; about sex and random things, never about anything important. "Is it weird to have me here working?"

"I already said no, but if you keep mentioning it, then I'm going to think that you think it's weird."

A warm rush of blood spread over Elle's face. "You have a good point."

"I know. I'm all about good ideas." Charlie's smile heated up the room.

"Great ones too."

"Fuck, I miss kissing you." Charlie pounced before Elle had time to adjust and prepare herself. For what? For an incredible kiss that felt like home. She didn't need to prepare herself for that, she only needed to fall into it. Into bliss.

The subtle rose of Charlie's perfume surrounded Elle and she drew the fragrance deep into her lungs. Elle kissed Charlie with all the longing of missed time. It'd been forever since she'd kissed Charlie and she poured herself into the kiss. She slowed the urgency of their mouths, crushed together, and relaxed to make the kiss more languid. Sweet nips of lips and darting strokes of her tongue over Charlie until heat blossomed between them. Elle pressed her body against Charlie, slowly moving her until Charlie was cushioned between Elle and the wall. Just like the first time, so long ago. And just like then, this didn't have to mean anything. It was the hook up of old lovers, comfortable with each other's bodies and pleasure. Elle knew what Charlie liked and she intended to give and take with the same ease.

"Touch me," Charlie breathed urgently into their kiss, the words muffled by their proximity, but Elle knew what she meant. She pushed her hand between them, cupping Charlie's mound. The zip of her jeans was rough against her palm and Charlie's eyes widened and darkened. Elle blinked for a second, unable to believe that she was here, ready to fuck Charlie in the middle of the afternoon where anyone could walk past.

"Someone might see." She pulled back a fraction.

Charlie grinned. "Isn't that exciting?"

"Um, yeah, sure."

"If it's not for you, we can stop."

Elle didn't want to stop. "Can we go somewhere more private?"

"People hardly ever walk this way."

Elle swallowed. "I'm not an exhibitionist like you."

"Ouch." Charlie slid sideways away from Elle, with her hand pressed to her chest, and Elle's breath stuck in her lungs. Shit. Just as Elle was about to open her mouth and apologise profusely, Charlie laughed.

"Oh shit, you should see your face. I miss the fuck out of teasing you. You always fall for stuff like that."

"I happen to like consent with my hook ups." Elle wanted to put her hands on her hips and glare, but that seemed to be too obviously falling into Charlie's nonsense.

"So now I'm an exhibitionist who doesn't care for consent. Careful." Charlie grinned and tilted her head to the side, so Elle at least had a clue that this was the teasing continuing.

She shook her head slowly.

"Damn you. You know when I first saw you up on that stage, I couldn't understand how doing burlesque was empowering, but fucking look at you. You've survived all this time and you are still amazing."

"Fabulous, darling. I'm fucking fabulous." Charlie threw her head back and laughed.

Elle wanted to capture the sound and keep it forever. It was the easiest thing in the world to fling her arms around Charlie's shoulders and kiss her. Deeply, passionately, and with zero regard for the fact that they might be seen by someone. Charlie's boldness could be hers. Because damn it, Elle was a successful businessperson now, not the downtrodden accounts manager at a shitty office furniture sales company. She had earned great sex with a fun partner. Charlie. Elle was a success and she'd bloody well demonstrate her new-found brilliance to Charlie.

Decision made, Elle bent over and took off her shoes. "Come here. Get on your knees and spread your legs." She bit her lip as Charlie obeyed, then Elle walked to stand between Charlie's thighs.

"Now what?"

Elle licked her dry lips—she would do this and it didn't matter who might see them—and she slowly pulled down her trousers and panties so she was bare from the waist down. "Kiss me." She leaned forward against the wall. At least the wall would hide the furious blush that made her face blazing hot. Then Charlie nuzzled against her bare pussy and the surroundings disappeared. Everything focused on how Charlie's tongue flicked across her clit.

Elle groaned. "Fuck yes. I've missed you." She stretched out and welcomed the way Charlie caressed the back of her thighs and gripped her bottom. "Harder."

Charlie covered her with her mouth and Elle's knees weakened as Charlie savoured her with a decent tongue lashing.

"That's indecent," Elle managed to croak out a few words of encouragement, ones that worked as Charlie's fingers dug into her flesh and her tongue and lips created pleasure in her core. Every lick had Elle pressing her palms harder against the wall, needing to hold on tight before her knees weakened. She used her toes to help support her, with the added benefit that Charlie moaned as Elle's toes pushed up against her tight jeans. Soon, Elle's thighs trembled and when Charlie nipped at her clit, she came undone with her eyes closed and her hands sliding on the rough wall of the hallway. Fireworks surrounded her as waves of wonderful spasms flowed through her body.

"Holy fuck, Charlie. I—" She couldn't form any more words as Charlie's urgent tongue gave her no reprieve. She bucked and cried out, over and over, until she sank to the floor and Charlie held her tight.

"I missed you." Elle found the last of her energy and kissed Charlie. The kiss was different to before, softer, with the taste of herself on Charlie's lips and Charlie's arms around her shoulders, holding her tight.

"I love it when you order me around, and then come completely undone." How could Charlie manage to talk right now? All Elle wanted to do was cuddle into Charlie and close her eyes. An alarm sounded and she blinked.

"Shit." They were back stage at Seraph's in the middle of the day where anyone could walk past and she'd been so lost in being tongue fucked by Charlie that she sat here with her pants around her ankles and only Charlie's arms protecting her.

"Yeah, that's my class alarm. I'd better go."

Elle scrambled to her feet and pulled up her trousers.

"Slow down, it's okay." Charlie rose to her feet and helped Elle with her pants. "You really are delightful."

"Why?" Elle shouldn't ask. She closed her eyes, not wanting to see Charlie's expression.

"Because you are so commanding, and then so awkward. It's like you get lost in the moment and show me your real self, then you pull on your barriers again and hide."

Elle straightened her top and patted her hair. "Thanks. I guess I'll see you around." She bolted down the hallway before she admitted how close Charlie had gotten to the truth. Sometimes sex was the only place that she truly felt like herself, a bolder version of herself, someone she wanted to be. An aspiration. Even now as the owner of a successful business, Elle still had to work to overcome her natural hesitancy. As she paced away, she realised she owed Charlie an orgasm. She skipped and let out a wild giggle. This wouldn't be their last time.

5

Charlie was still buzzing when she walked—skipped—into work the next day. After initially assuming she'd messed up, she'd ended up with incredible stolen moments spent kissing Elle until she came all over her face. There was something extra about the way Elle balanced all the facets of herself; it'd never be boring being with her. The way she stressed about being in a hallway where anyone could see them, then with a little teasing, she'd made the fucking stunning decision to strip off her pants and bare herself, not just to Charlie, but to anyone who might walk down the narrow space connecting the rooms behind the stage. The audacity in her deliberate choice was enough to have Charlie lingering on the edge of an orgasm even before she'd tasted Elle on her tongue. During the pandemic lockdowns, Charlie had missed Elle's clean musk and delicious taste and her first taste again hadn't disappointed. Unlike everything else. The sheer relief that something was still as good as before overwhelmed her with joy.

Without any time to process what had happened, Charlie

had bounced into her dance class, and it'd been the best, most energetic session she'd had in ages. Yes, being with Elle made all aspects of her life better. Could she admit that aloud yet? No. Instead she'd focused on work. The photography session with Sarah went well; she had chosen the correct size for herself and Ben's photos were stunning. He brought out the depth of Sarah's brown skin and the headdress they'd picked made her black hair look so luxurious. Charlie wanted to see Elle wear the same outfit because her black hair had the same potential; except better because it was Elle.

Charlie dumped her bag on her desk and turned on the computer, ready to plan the next month's events with a fresh upbeat positivity. She'd missed feeling like this. Her phone rang. Mum. With a deep breath that did nothing to ease the sudden tension caused by seeing her mum's name on her phone screen, she answered. As ever, the timing sucked most of the joy out of her lungs.

"Hi Mum." Once again, years of acting training came in handy as she managed to sound upbeat.

"Charlotte, darling." Oh fuck, that tone didn't bode well.

"What do you want?"

"Why would you ask such a thing? Don't you want to know how I am?"

"Fine. How are you, Mum?"

"I'm great. Do you remember Tom Scottridge?"

Charlie rolled her eyes. The whole fucking world knew Tom Scottridge; Oscar winner, silver fox, heart throb to the world's middle-aged women and many others too. "The actor?"

"Yes. I'm going to be working with him on a new project."

Shit, that was massive news. "Congratulations, Mum."

Charlie didn't have to pretend to be pleased for her. A project with Tom Scottridge was a huge coup for her C-grade soap opera career.

"Thanks. So I thought we'd come along tonight and watch your show."

Charlie choked on her own spit. "Excuse me?"

Her mother had never come to any of her shows because having her there would apparently only encourage Charlie to keep dancing. Supposedly, burlesque was beneath her talents, and apparently Charlie ought to be working alongside her on TV. Charlie had grown up on soap opera sets. It wasn't a life she wanted for herself. Burlesque was her own space, on stage, away from her mother's life, a place she could showcase her abilities without judgement and all the snide politics that came with struggling actors bickering over roles.

"Yes. It's been so much fun to spend time with dear Tom again. Did you know we worked together on 'Red Roses Of The Plains' before you were born?" Her mother had a bit part on the show and from there, she'd gained the role of the elegant private school headmistress in Chelsea Avenue, a long running soap opera, where she'd been ever since.

"Yes, Mum. You mention that every time we see a headline of his." Which was often because the actor was everywhere. He was literally one of the biggest actors in the world, making a pile of high earning movies with his chiselled jaw and upper class British accent. Charlie had never really understood the appeal. Tom Scottridge was the epitome of the bland white actor that looked like about ten other actors; dark blonde hair, blue eyes, generally pleasing features. To be fair to the guy, Charlie didn't find many men attractive, and when she did, her type tended towards people who were less model-like and more interesting.

"Well, he is your father, so it's only natural that I'd mention him often."

Charlie gaped at her phone. What the fucking hell? Mum had never mentioned THAT fact before. She couldn't speak or breathe. Fucking what?

"And since we are about to work together again, I thought it might be fun if we were seen out and about together. Naturally, we would come to support you, even if he won't want it mentioned that you are related to him."

"Right." Because an actor of his level couldn't possibly have a burlesque dancer as a daughter. She was too stunned to actually say that aloud. Charlie thought her eyes might fall out of her head. Shit. Fuck. What was worse? Her mother coming to watch her, just casually mentioning her father was bloody Tom Scottridge. She'd never ever mentioned that before. And… And they were both coming to watch her tonight.

Nope. There was no fucking way she was going to perform in front of her mum and her alleged father, who happened to be the biggest fucking name in acting, not just right now but for the last decade. Shit, shit. Thank fuck to the heavens that she'd never lusted after him. How fucking awkward would be to have a memory of his poster on her walls as a teenager or some shit? At least she'd spared herself that misery. She wanted to hide under her kitchen table or stand in Hyde Park and scream to the sky or something. Anything but this.

"It's not about that. He's very high profile now and we are about to embark on a new project, and he doesn't want it derailed."

"Hold on. Are you saying that he knows about me?"

"Always has."

Hold on, what? Charlie's brain must lack oxygen because did her mum just say that Tom Scottridge knew about her this whole time? What an asshole, ignoring her like that. Charlie had been okay with never knowing who her father was. She'd always vaguely assumed Mum had picked someone from a sperm bank.

"We agreed to keep it secret from the press. How do you think I could afford all those dance and acting classes for you?" The nasty revelations kept coming.

"And was the deal that you didn't tell me?" She was so stunned that not a shred of bitterness came through in her tone. A tiny taste of lemon peel painted her tongue—the hurt would come soon. This was like being abandoned without knowing it.

"Darling. It's not like that. I couldn't tell anyone."

"Including me?"

"Anyone."

"So yes, including me. Fine. Whatever, Mum. I'll see you both tonight." Charlie hung up before she said something she regretted.

Luckily Charlie had never done anything that might be fucking weird thanks to not having that rather crucial piece of information. Like, she had never met the guy, so at least she hadn't accidentally hit on her own father, but she'd also never lusted after photos of the guy or anything like that. Tom Scottridge was everywhere; it was a miracle she'd never been drawn into discussions on how hot (or not) he was. Her bloody mother deserved a tongue lashing over this—maybe one day—except she was all the family she'd ever had, and for all her selfish faults, she was still her mum.

One thing was true. There was no way Charlie was dancing tonight. She paced around the room trying to figure out this whole thing. Tom Scottridge was her father. She opened the search app on her phone and googled him. Yes, he'd definitely worked with her mum in the same year that she'd been conceived. It was unlikely that it was one of Mum's stories. She called her mum back, who answered on the first ring.

"One question."

"My darling Charlotte. I'm always here to answer your questions." Well, that was bullshit, but sure … Charlie could work with it right at this second.

"I suppose I can't tell anyone either."

"That would be best."

"What does that mean?"

Mum sighed, theatrically, because that's how she did everything. "Technically and legally, I signed the non-disclosure form and I get the monthly payment if it stays secret. The only thing stopping you from mentioning it is that it will end my payment from him. And I'm sure you wouldn't want that."

"I'm sure that's true." If she were a meaner person, she'd see opportunity in that. Okay, so she saw opportunity anyway, but she wasn't going to do anything about it. Long ago, she'd decided not to behave in the same way Mum did. The times when she had any instinctive thoughts around manipulating a situation, she pulled herself up and stopped before acting. "Why tell me then?"

"Darling girl. You look just like him. I wanted to warn you in case someone saw the three of us together and figured it out. I would hate for you to learn it from the press, and not me, even though I'm in breach of contract by telling you."

And it would okay if the press guessed? Mum would probably make the most of that situation; the gossip rags could talk about it for months with both her and Tom—Tom Scottridge!—denying it, while they both gained loads of publicity for their new project. What did it matter? Her little scheme to have them all seen together wasn't going to do anything because the idea that Charlie looked like him? Nah. She had the same dirty blonde hair, but so did lots of people. She had Mum's brown eyes, much to Mum's horror. Imagine if she'd had blue eyes, she would've been given bigger roles, blah blah.

"Okay." The convoluted logic almost made sense. She should warn Beth and Walter, their security guy, that Tom Scottridge might attend tonight. Fuck. If she did that, she'd have to tell them how she knew. She'd think of something. "Okay. Thanks. I'll see you tonight, Mum."

She threw her phone on the table and paced around her office, but it was too small. Maybe she could put on some loud music in the warm up room and throw her body around a bit with something energetic.

~

"What the hell?" Beth turned down the thumping bass heavy music. "What is going on?"

"Um, I have some news." Charlie pulled herself off the floor and stood up. She couldn't talk about Tom being her father, but she could at least tell Beth about her Mum. Decision made. And if she said that Mum was bringing Tom, that wasn't technically a lie.

"News that requires you to blast the sound system?"

"Yes. So did I ever tell you that my Mum is an actress?" Charlie gulped.

"No. Who?"

"Lottie Alcott-James." She shared the same name as Mum —Charlotte Kent—and as usual she sent a quick thanks to Mum for using a stage name because telling people that her mum was Lottie Kent usually didn't connect her to the soap opera actress. It was also quite handy in the rest of her life as people didn't continually say, oh just like the actress?

"Sylvia Wood from Chelsea Avenue?"

"Yes. So um, anyway, she's coming tonight to watch the show, and she's bringing a… um, work colleague of hers." Charlie hated the uncertainty in her voice, her arms, her everything and she stiffened her spine and painted on a more confident expression.

Beth nodded. "Okay. Are you planning to dance?"

"No. I'm going to find someone to fill in for my slot and I'll just do the MC-ing tonight. I know everyone else will notice that I'm not dancing and will ask about why. Can you make up something? I don't particularly want everyone to know who my mum is."

"Cool. I'll keep your secret. I've kept Reiko's for the best part of a decade now."

Charlie raised one eyebrow. "Reiko has a secret?" She breathed out. "Never mind. Everyone has secrets. Um, maybe it doesn't matter if everyone knows who my mum is."

"It'll be easier to explain why you aren't dancing tonight?"

Charlie nodded. "Yes. Okay. Just as long as no one is weird about it."

"I think you'll find that our crew will be more supportive than you imagine."

"Yeah, it's not like she's super famous." Charlie gasped. Shit. "Speaking of famous, um, don't you want to know who Mum is bringing with her?"

"Sure. I assume it's someone famous."

"Um. Yeah." Charlie cleared her throat. "It's Tom Scottridge."

"Who?"

Charlie laughed. "Seriously?" Maybe it wouldn't be so bad if anyone ever found out he was her father.

Beth wrinkled her nose and grinned, and Charlie belatedly realised Beth had been teasing. "I might be a bisexual person who leans towards being lesbian, but I still watch the occasional het movie. They're a bit hard to avoid. So yes, I know who Tom Scottridge is."

"Right. Yeah."

"Is your Mum dating Tom Scottridge?"

Charlie opened her mouth then closed it again. Damn, she'd nearly said, not anymore. "Um…" She cleared her throat. "No, well, Mum hasn't said and it's the kind of thing she would boast about, so I assume no. They are apparently working on a project together."

"I take it the press will follow him?"

Charlie shrugged. "I don't know. Mum literally called me half an hour ago with this news, and that's all I know."

"Okay. You need to stop drowning your emotions in loud music and find a replacement dancer for your slot tonight."

"Yes." Charlie nodded, glad to have something constructive to do. She would've done it without Beth's instruction. It was just … useful to have someone remind her of her priorities.

"It's cool. I'll let Walter know he might need to plan for

the press tonight." Beth turned up the music and left Charlie to it. The heat had gone out of her, so she walked over to the stereo and changed the music to her usual stretching playlist. She changed the volume to match and went through her routine. Each stretch helped ground her back into real life; work, dancing, organising. Who could she call at this last minute? And if she didn't find anyone, could she just shorten the program tonight? Would anyone notice? Probably not. Oh… Yolande and Jack had been practicing a new dance together. Maybe they'd give it a test run tonight?

6

E lle rubbed her eyes. She'd been staring at her computer screen for hours trying to figure out how to take the jumbled plan at Seraph's and rework it into a functional design. Hours, days, whatever. She needed to take a break and stare at some nature or something in the distance to rest her eyes. It'd been a few days since she'd stripped off her pants and Charlie had tongue-fucked her in the hallway at Seraph's. She shivered.

What was it about Charlie? Elle never shed her inhibitions with anyone else, and yet one teasing word from Charlie and she'd bared herself in public where anyone might walk past. She swallowed and leaned back in her chair. Her hand drifted down over the soft fabric of her shirt as it stretched across her belly to the waistband of her trackpants. Working from home had a few benefits. Elle slipped her hand inside her trackpants and pressed her clit. Fucking hell, just thinking about Charlie's tongue on her and the way she'd held Elle's bare arse as she'd licked her until she'd come made Elle moan. She was wet just thinking about how she'd bit her lip hard to stop herself crying out.

Somehow taking a risk and being vulnerably naked in public with Charlie's hands on her arse and her tongue inside her had made the whole experience sharper, more desperate, than it would've been in a private space where no one would ever interrupt them. Charlie pushed her beyond her limits and she fucking adored it, adored her. Elle sucked in a deep breath and pinched her clit. What a naughty girl she was. Pressure built up and she rubbed harder and harder until she came; right there in her office chair, in front of her computer screen.

For a second, she held her breath and quickly scanned the screen. No, she didn't have any meeting apps open; thank fuck, she didn't have to deal with that particular humiliation. It was practically its own genre of internet joke now. She'd loved the one of the woman talking in a meeting and her boyfriend had walked into the screenshot. The woman waved him away, and he'd freaked out and run right into a wall and collapsed. There were other ones, but none tickled her the same as that one. The poor dude had obviously been trying so hard to not distract her from her work.

She chuckled as she wandered across her flat to wash her hands. Maybe she'd go to Seraph's tonight and see if Charlie was around? Her phone rang and she dried her hands as she paced back towards her desk to grab it.

"Hi."

"Elle, how are you?" Willow's enthusiastic voice shrill in her ear.

"I'm good."

"Awesome. Are you coming to Joey's birthday party this weekend?"

Elle rolled her eyes. As if she could possibly forget ... Willow posted about Joey online every day. At least once a week Elle contemplated blocking her for a few days just to get away from Willow's perfectly curated #mumlife.

"Of course. Remind me of his favourite colour again." Last week, it'd been blue, but from what Willow said, Joey tended to change his mind a lot. As Willow rambled on about Joey, something about how he'd missed his first birthday party because of the pandemic, Elle let her mind wander. The first draft of plans for Seraph's would be done soon and she had a meeting with Beth in a couple of days to go over them and run through the initial costing. The plans could be built within budget, and as long as Beth liked the plans, then everything could smoothly progress into the build stage of the refitting project. Seraph's was her first commercial space design and it was a huge challenge compared to all the residential houses she'd done since starting her business.

"You aren't listening, are you?"

"Sorry."

"I said, do you think Hugh would prefer the dark red or the dark blue tie? I sent you the pictures."

Elle shrugged. "I have no clue what my brother would want."

"It's important. I don't want to get it wrong." Willow's usually upbeat voice had an odd tone to it, one that Elle had spent a lot of time trying not to remember.

"Willow." How could she say this? "Why are you selecting his tie?"

"I told you already. He has a big meeting tomorrow and he wanted me to buy him a new tie to go with his navy suit, but I can't decide if a matching tie is too boring or if the red is too much."

"Buy both and he can choose."

"Oh no, you know what he is like. He trusts my opinion on fashion, so I have to decide." Confidence returned to Willow's voice.

"Willow, he's not going to fail in a meeting if he wears the wrong tie. Ask him what kind of impression he wants to make. Does he want to appear—" Elle couldn't say boring about her own brother even if it was a little true, "—um, consistent and like he fits in with the general business crowd? Then use the blue. Or does he want to look like a creative thinker who will bring ideas to the table? The red would be best for that."

"Thank you. That's what I was missing. I will ask him. We'll see you on Saturday, then?"

"Yes." Elle said her goodbyes and hung up. Shit. She hated the way her heart pumped and the sense of vigilance that surrounded her; she didn't want to go to Joey's party and watch her brother closely just in case he had become too concerned with his image ... No, he wouldn't. He knew what it was like. Speaking of ... that, she needed to get this design done for Seraph's and update her spreadsheet.

Elle didn't need to look at it to know how many more jobs she had to make a profit on before she'd repaid her parents their seed money. That figure was branded in the forefront of everything she did. She hadn't wanted to ask them to help her get her business started. She had worked for years in a crappy job to avoid their involvement in her business, but in the end, she'd negotiated a reasonably sized loan so she could get away from her old boring job that was stealing her creativity and motivation. She'd needed to start her business more than she'd needed to avoid being in debt to her parents. And it'd been—mostly—worth it.

The sooner she'd focused on work, the sooner she'd be able to cancel that debt and be free again. She needed to get more marketing happening to get her goal achieved faster It'd been a few days since she'd posted anything on her business social media pages. Her employee Susan did most of the social media stuff and was much better at it than Elle, especially at the engaging with people part of it. Too many people asked the same boring questions over and over and most of them never bought anything. Yes, she knew social media wasn't technically all about sales. This was her business though, and it was hard —impossible—not to worry about the bottom line. Especially when a quick conversation with her sister-in-law reminded her that she'd see her parents this weekend, and she still owed them money. She slid into her office chair and opened an internet browser window.

"Tom Scottridge's secret love child." The headline screamed at her in bold letters and she sighed. She really ought to change the automated setting from the news to her own website. Hold on. She squinted at the screen. Was that a blurry picture of Charlie? No. It couldn't be. Except it really did look like her. She picked up her phone to send her a message, then put it back on her desk. For all the times they'd hooked up, they'd never swapped phone numbers. She had no way to call Charlie and see if she was okay. Her toes tapped on the ground. Eventually a solution came. Beth. Was it weird to ask her client if Charlie was okay? Yes, most likely. What about Yolande or Reiko? They worked with Charlie.

Elle: Hey Reiko. Is Charlie okay? She hit send before she

could second guess herself, but the thoughts flooded her in an ugly loop. Why didn't she explain why she was asking?

Reiko: I take it you've seen the news.

Elle: Yes.

Her phone rang. "Hi Reiko. How is she?"

"I'm annoyed as fuck." Charlie made a sound that was somewhere between a laugh and a strangled cry. It took Elle a second; Charlie must using Reiko's phone to call her after the text she'd sent.

"Why? I mean, are you okay?" Silly question; using Reiko's phone wasn't exactly a sign that all was well.

Charlie laughed, a mean hard laugh. "I'm fine. Obviously, since I'm hiding at Reiko's place to avoid the piles of paparazzi outside my flat and Seraph's."

"Right. I'm glad you are safe." Elle swallowed. She really didn't have this type of relationship with Charlie where they talked about … well, anything real.

"Thanks."

"Is there anything I can do?"

"Punch my mother."

Elle gasped. "Excuse me."

"Never mind." Charlie's sigh vibrated in her ear. "Mum wanted some publicity for her new movie and it kind of blew up."

Elle rubbed her forehead. "Your mum is an actress?"

"Yeah, she plays Sylvie Wood on Chelsea Avenue."

"The soap opera?"

"Yeah, that one."

Elle had way too many questions, but none of them mattered right now. "I'm sorry that you've been dragged into this."

"I'm used to it." Charlie sighed again. "I mean, not the whole Scottridge nonsense but you know, Mum has been on that show since I was a toddler, so it's kind of normal to me to see pictures of me in the news."

"Of you?"

Charlie clicked her tongue. "It was worse when I was a kid. Mum loved the photo shoot opportunities, you know, hard working solo mum actress, blah blah."

Elle didn't buy the blasé way Charlie talked. Was it really her business if Charlie wanted to pretend that everything was okay? "Do you want to…"

"Meet. Yes, I need to get rid of some of this energy."

Heat shot down Elle's spine. "Where?" She had been thinking they'd have coffee and they'd talk or something, but this was more like their usual thing. They connected physically, and if Charlie needed Elle to fuck her senseless to make her feel better, then Elle would be there. She wanted to be the one who Charlie used when she needed release.

"Can you come here? I can't really leave without being mobbed at the moment."

"I assume you are at Reiko and Yolande's apartment?"

"Yes. I'll text you the address."

She already had their address because she'd decorated the whole apartment. Elle bit her lip. "What about…? Um, we won't be alone."

"They can leave for a while."

"While we hook up? Isn't that weird?"

"Fucking yes, it's weird. So weird. Everything about this is weird."

Elle wanted to kiss Charlie's anguish away. "Tell me a time and I'll be there."

"Okay." Charlie hung up, leaving Elle standing in her office. She wasn't going to be able to focus on work now. Maybe she'd go for a swim in the lap pool in her apartment building. It'd probably be empty at this time of day. Her phone beeped with an incoming text. It was from a number she didn't recognise.

"Come now."

Elle almost dropped her phone. There was no doubt that the text came from Charlie and even less doubt about her next action. She stripped off her clothes as she walked to the bathroom; somehow managing to get there without injuring herself in her rush to wash and get ready to go to Charlie. As she waited for the water to warm up, she scratched her head. Would she ever reconcile her need to please in real life with her need to command during sex? Oh—she knew precisely where the need to please came from … Heat prickled the corners of her eyes and she jumped into the shower, letting the water wash away the sudden tears. One day she'd come to terms with never being good enough for her parents. It was one of those complicated situations. They'd never abused her or anything. On the face of it, they were a perfect family. Father, mother, one son, and one daughter, who all went to church in their village every Sunday. Her mum volunteered for almost everything in the village, and Dad was the town's accountant. It was all very ordinary. She had nothing to complain about; not compared to the situations she read about in the news. There was always someone worse off than her, and if she couldn't cope with a little criticism from her parents, then she must be weak. She bowed her head under the water. She wasn't weak. She'd work harder to prove it to them. Soon her debt to them would be repaid. She was on target for repaying it earlier than they expected. That had to be worth some praise. She turned her face upwards and let the water stream over her, washing away the tears that refused to stop. Screw them. Right now, she had somewhere more important to be. She'd go to Charlie and give her the escape she'd asked for.

L ess than an hour later, Elle pushed the buzzer to Reiko and Yolande's apartment. The simple sign didn't have a name on it and for good reason. Aside from the fact that Reiko didn't like people knowing that she was from the Inoue Media family, this was the type of expensive apartment building where everyone valued their privacy and anonymity.

"Come."

Elle didn't have a chance to say something cheeky, like 'I intend to', because the door beeped and she needed to push it open and enter the building. The lift in the lobby had a no-touch system, and she sanitised her hands while she waited until one of the elevators opened. It took her directly to the penthouse suite. There were only two apartments on this floor; one decorated in a lush soft style chosen by Reiko and Yolande with a purpose built cat play area and house for their cats, Captain and Bounce. The other had a stark minimalist decorative style to suit the wealthy owner who occasionally stayed there when in London. She'd designed both places; Reiko had kindly offered to get her father to feature her place in an article, and the PA for the owner of the other apartment, Georgie, had contacted her about his place. She still didn't know the owner's name, only one of his company names, Beautravers Investments, because that's who she'd been told to invoice.

Georgie hadn't given away many clues either, except to say her boss travelled a lot for work and he would approve everything via email. Whatever. It'd been a great challenge to take what was essentially the same space and design two very different interiors to suit the owners.

She stepped out of the lift and knocked on the front door for the apartment. After a long minute, Elle's toes started to jiggle in her shoe until Charlie, finally, opened the door. The white top she wore stole Elle's breath away; it was tight with lacing that drew her gaze to Charlie's tits.

"Come in."

Elle swallowed. "Come now. Come. Come in." She repeated all of Charlie's various comments, ones that had cycled around her head as she'd sat on the tube on the way here, trying to distract herself with the latest Fiona Zedde erotica. It had only left her needy and desperate to see Charlie, who stood in front of her with her tits right there. A shiver raced down her spine and she was already wet and ready.

"Yes. What took you so long?"

"I live at Crouch End." Elle lifted her gaze up from Charlie's tits. The little smirk on Charlie's lips sent a flush of heat across Elle's cheeks.

"If you want to touch these—" Charlie shook her tits a little, "—you'll need to follow me." She spun around and walked into Reiko and Yolande's apartment. Elle gasped. Charlie wore black fishnet stockings on her long legs with a seam line that ran up the back of her legs from her red stilettos all the way up to her arse. The world's tiniest g-string in matching red was barely visible under the fishnets thanks to the colour, and of course, when Elle finally moved her feet to follow Charlie inside, Charlie slapped her hands on her arse.

Oh. Elle couldn't hold back the moan. The door closed behind her with a quiet click. Elle licked her dry lips.

"You don't have to dance for me." Her voice sounded like it'd been dragged along a gravel road behind a motorbike.

Charlie glanced over her shoulder. "What if I want to?"

"I wouldn't say no."

"Sit." Charlie pointed to a chair and Elle sat, barely noticing anything except Charlie. They could've been in a basement, or on a beach, or anywhere, and Elle wouldn't have seen anything except Charlie. Charlie, who leaned forward seductively, in a deliberate burlesque move that Elle had seen her do on stage a million times. Why was it so much hotter when it was just for her? Her tits spilled against the gap in the top she wore, and Elle's fingers itched to pull it off.

"Take it off." Elle found her voice, although it grumbled under a groan as Charlie shook her tits again. How did she do that without moving her shoulders?

"Patience. Don't you know that burlesque is all about the tease?"

"Maybe I don't want to be teased. Maybe I just want to rip off those stockings and lick you."

Charlie pursed her lips. "Maybe I'd let you…" She smirked a little, "—except I haven't danced for a week thanks to the fucking disaster that is my mother's life."

"I can help you forget." Elle could kiss all that frustration away until Charlie cried out for her.

"How?" Charlie walked towards her, slowly pulling her top upward, exposing her taut belly. She stopped a few inches away from Elle, close enough that Elle could see the way gooseflesh rose on Charlie's skin as she blew a long breath over Charlie's belly button.

"Keep doing that and you'll find out."

"And if I turn away?"

Elle grinned. "Try it."

Charlie turned slowly—so slowly—then bent forward so her arse was right in front of Elle's face. Elle leaned forward on the chair and did the most obvious thing. She licked right between Charlie's legs, tasting only fabric at first, and then, yes, Charlie's wetness coated her tongue and she licked again. The little hint of rose came through under the overwhelming perfection of Charlie. The fabric rasped on her tongue, opposite to the soft texture of Charlie's skin.

"I thought you were going to rip them off first."

Elle chuckled against Charlie's g-string and licked her again. She gripped the edge of the chair to stop herself using her hands; she wanted Charlie to keep herself there of her own choice.

"Go on."

Elle licked again and this time, Charlie was even wetter. The fabric didn't have the best texture but it didn't matter, the taste of Charlie dominated. "You do it. You wanted to dance."

Charlie only groaned in reply, then slowly pulled her shirt over her head and dropped it on the ground beside her. She bent her spine and spread her legs a little more, so Elle had to change the angle of her head to keep her mouth against Charlie's sex.

"There's too much fabric here."

"Patience." The word was almost lost in the moan from Charlie, and Elle wanted to make her do it again.

"Or…" She stretched higher on the chair so her chin rested on the top of Charlie's arse. "Or…" She waited, purposefully, to see how Charlie would react. Charlie jumped forwards, leaving a whisper of cool air and without somewhere to rest her chin, Elle nearly toppled forward off the chair. Good thing she was clinging on with her hands. Charlie spun around. Her tits looked great in a matching red bra with lace edging.

Elle twisted her hands together in her lap; better that than reach up and grope Charlie. She wanted Charlie to decide their pace today because it was Charlie's need who mattered most after being hounded by the press. How stressful. Charlie wriggled her hips and slid the stockings down over her g-string. With the waistband hooked around the top of her thighs, she danced, slowly gyrating and twisting. As much as Elle appreciated the performance, she had Charlie's taste on her tongue and she wanted more.

"That's enough." Elle stood up and marched over to Charlie. She reached up, slinging her arms around Charlie's shoulders, and pulled her down for a kiss. Elle kissed her hungrily. She'd missed this, the tangle of their tongues, the way Charlie danced in a kiss, always teasing and taunting, and yet, when Elle pushed, Charlie gave way perfectly.

Together they lowered to the couch, mouths still tangled, and Elle couldn't hold back a sigh as she lay on top of Charlie. She could just stay there, pressed against her gorgeous body, but she knew that Charlie needed more than that.

"How long have you been stuck here?"

"A couple of days. The press followed me home after work and wouldn't leave. Reiko rescued me."

Elle grinned. "She's such a good friend." She kissed Charlie again.

"Yeah. I don't want to think about it now. Not with you and your curves all over me."

Elle flushed. She swallowed back the question filled with doubt about her body and sucked in a deep breath. Why doubt when Charlie obviously wanted her? She kissed her again, deep and passionate, until Charlie groaned into her mouth. It was so easy to nibble along Charlie's jaw, down her throat, and press a kiss to the hollow between her collar bones. She held Charlie's face, then slowly and deliberately used her fingers to trail after her kisses. With a wriggle, she shifted off the couch to kneel on the floor. It gave her more space to explore Charlie's incredible body.

"So fit and strong."

"Benefits of the job." Charlie winked with that little smirk on her lips again. Elle reached up and pressed her fingers against Charlie's lips.

"Shh." Uncertainty still plagued her, something that didn't usually happen in the presence of Charlie and her amazing body. Maybe it was the change of location; she'd never fucked Charlie anywhere except at Seraph's and always after a show … Except for the other day. This would be the second exception. She should just embrace this. Embrace Charlie. What was stopping her?

7

Charlie understood patience. The art of burlesque was all about anticipation, building people up and making them wait for the final moment. And never quite giving it to them. So she waited, with Elle's fingers on her lips. The gentle touch wasn't enough to keep her in place. Elle's command was. She wanted to see what Elle would do next. One of the reasons Elle was her favourite hook up was her vast imagination. Charlie only had to wait long enough for Elle to cast off her uncertainty, the shield of caution that she carried with her, and step into herself. Because when Elle decided what she wanted, it was incredibly hot.

The change in her demeanour was like watching a shape-shifter turn from a timid human into a bold lioness in charge of the herd. When Elle knew what she wanted, she became a queen. The commander of Charlie's body. Charlie wanted that more than anything; to lose herself in Elle's directions with all of Elle's focus on her. It was like being on stage, but with only one person in the audience, with all the intensity that came from that. Too many hook ups let their minds drift during sex, and Charlie could tell when they weren't fully committed.

Elle never did that. The silence from Elle stretched and stretched, and with each passing moment, Charlie became wetter. She wanted to rip off her stupid stockings. Why did she choose ones that went up to her waist over single legs ones with a garter belt? Garters were hotter. Her mouth dried out and still Elle didn't move. Charlie groaned, needing something.

"Shh." Elle stared, casting her gaze up and down Charlie's torso, leaving spots of heat as if she'd touched her. Hopefully Elle was planning where she would kiss Charlie. *There, yes, right there.* She'd already had her mouth on her and Charlie wanted more.

Charlie lifted her hips, rolling her pelvis slightly so she wasn't flat on her back on the couch, but tilted towards Elle a little. The hint must have been enough as Elle puffed out a short breath, then leaned forward, placing one hand on Charlie's ankle and with her other hand, she slid her fingers down from Charlie's lips and pressed on the base of her throat. With Elle's hands spread out like that, her breasts brushed over Charlie's stomach and Charlie wanted to complain that Elle wore too many clothes. Instead, she pinched her lips together and Elle chuckled.

"Good." Elle inched her hand up Charlie's leg, tracing the squares of the fishnet stockings in random patterns, until she reached her knee. Damn it, Charlie had taught her the art of patience too much. Waves of heat flowed up her legs to the point where Elle's other hand rested lightly—too lightly—on her throat. She wanted to beg and writhe, and she pushed her spine against the couch to stay still. Her thighs started to tremble as Elle continued her anguished path up her skin. Elle plucked the stocking and let it fall with a little sting on her sensitive skin.

Charlie yelped.

"I thought I said shush."

Charlie nodded and held her lips tighter together. She adored this tension, and when Elle did it again, she held the yelp inside her mouth. Her skin flushed with heat, surely she would be pink all over by now, but she didn't want to look. Didn't want to see Elle's hands on her thighs. Feeling them was overwhelming enough.

She kept her gaze on the side of Elle's face, where the light from the huge windows created dancing shadows across Elle's light brown skin. A long time ago, Charlie hadn't been able to hold back her curiosity and during a memorable hook up, she'd asked about Elle's heritage. Her dad was white and her mum was third-generation English-born Indian. Elle had rolled her eyes at Charlie when she'd said nothing more and Charlie had stumbled over asking why she'd done that. The frustration in Elle's voice had been apparent when she'd talked about how people assumed her Mum didn't speak English properly, and how that discarded the long colonial history England had with India. Charlie had apologised and wished she hadn't asked the initial question; they didn't know each other that well, and Charlie had overstepped the boundary of their relationship, if it could be called that when it was a hook up. She'd never needed to explain her own white heritage in this country, no one ever asked, they just assumed she was from here.

Thinking about her own privilege while Elle literally stroked her skin into a furious fire created an odd juxtaposition in her brain. It couldn't be helped. Charlie was here thanks to the current fuss about her own parents. It was easy enough to remember a similar conversation and how she felt like she'd messed it up.

She shook off the thoughts. One thing she hated during sex was when the other person was obviously distracted or paying only some attention, and now she was doing just that. She blinked long and hard and focused on Elle's hands. The one at her throat pressed infinitesimally harder, not enough to restrict her breath, but certainly enough that Charlie noticed it. It felt like a thread connected Elle's hands, a long zap of electricity coursing between them, up and down her body, until she wanted to groan and pant and writhe.

Elle leaned forward and used her teeth to pull the waist-band of the stocking off Charlie's thighs where she'd pushed it down to earlier. Charlie held her breath, waiting for the inevitable slap of elastic on her skin. It didn't come. She waited and waited until she couldn't hold her breath anymore. She dragged in a heavy breath and only then did Elle let the elastic go. It pinged on Charlie's skin and she gasped. Elle hadn't said anything about not moving, so she grabbed her stockings and pushed them down her legs as far as she could reach. The elastic scratched her skin, surely leaving red marks behind, but she didn't care. She needed to be bare for Elle.

Elle's hands joined hers, stripping her of her stockings and g-string, and then Elle stood up. She pulled the stockings all the way down to Charlie's feet, then quickly undid her stilettos and took everything off. Charlie half sat up on her elbows, needing more, needing to watch what Elle was going to do next.

Elle hummed under her breath and Charlie wanted to beg

her to just pick something. To touch her. Anywhere. Elle licked her bottom lip and Charlie swallowed as the little pink slip of her tongue traced across her full lip. *Oh come on. Just touch already.*

Frustration built and her pulse beat unsteadily as her lungs craved more air. Elle tilted her head to the side, as if she were considering her options, and Charlie let out a strangled cry. On purpose. She wasn't allowed to talk or make noise, but she could still disobey and see what happened. She loved this game of ebb and flow between them. Elle grinned with the complete confidence of someone who knew she was playing with fire and did it deliberately. If Elle ever danced, she'd be the type who did fire-spinning or sword swallowing, something that risked physical danger. Just as Charlie was distracted, Elle moved. She knelt on the couch, one knee either side of Charlie's feet, and bent forward to cover Charlie's mound with her mouth. Charlie instinctively tried to spread her legs, but Elle had her legs trapped.

"Patience. Isn't that what you said?" Elle lifted her head away from where Charlie wanted it most and Charlie stared at her for a long moment until she did what Elle was obviously waiting for. She nodded.

"Then you should be able to take what you dish out."

Charlie's back arched in reflex. "Not fair."

"Shh." As Elle let the vibration of the word drift over Charlie's clit, Charlie bucked again. Fuck, she needed all of Elle's mouth on her. Temptation beckoned. She reached out and held Elle's head, letting her fingers spread through Elle's soft black strands.

"Charlie," Elle warned, but Charlie was done with her teasing. She pushed Elle's head down.

"Enough. Suck me now."

Elle laughed against Charlie's skin and the warm air made everything better. Elle followed the laugh with her tongue, licking and nipping and sucking, until Charlie moaned and cried out.

"Good. Make more noise. Show me your appreciation," Elle spoke with her chin pressed against Charlie's clit, then shifted to suck her again.

Charlie's grip on Elle's hair tightened, reflecting the pressure in her core, until she closed her eyes and let the waves of pleasure wash over her. Elle didn't stop, didn't give her any respite. She kissed and licked and nuzzled her as if she loved doing it and never wanted to stop. Charlie came and came, so hard that bright spots burst across her vision and she heard herself cry out over and over. Eventually Elle kissed Charlie's stomach and Charlie sank into the couch, her head resting somewhere soft with her eyes virtually rolled back in their sockets. All the drama and tension of the last few days was gone, whipped away by Elle's incredible tongue. Her limbs were heavy and she could barely keep her eyes open.

"Thanks." She managed to whisper before completely succumbing to her sated body's need for rest. The last thing she heard was Elle's quiet chuckle.

Charlie woke up with a grumble when someone shook her on the shoulder.

"Yolande and Reiko will be home soon. You might want to get dressed." Elle. Charlie rubbed her eyes. What? Oh. She gasped. Elle was here. They'd had great sex, except she'd fallen asleep before Elle had come and now her pulse raced for all the wrong reasons.

"I'm so sorry."

"For?"

"Not making you come."

Elle grinned. "I'm good. I sorted myself out after covering you with a blanket."

"A blanket?" There was a blanket over here, a soft one that had to be made from some incredibly expensive material because it was somehow heavy and comforting and so soft against her skin. Like a fucking warm cloud or something.

"Yeah. I didn't want you to get cold, and I thought it might be a bit creepy to rub myself while you were sleeping, so I covered you up first."

"Um, thanks. It would've been fine." Charlie loved the idea that Elle would get off to her body.

"No."

"Would it be okay if I was awake?"

Elle raised one eyebrow. "Do you mean, would it be okay if I masturbated while watching you pretend to sleep?"

"Yes." There would be no pretence of sleep. Charlie really wanted to see Elle exposed and exploring herself. "I want to watch."

Elle's face glowed with a bright red blush. "Not today. Yolande and Reiko will be here soon."

"But sometime?"

Elle closed her eyes for a second and when she opened them again, she sent Charlie the most intense look. "Yes. Sometime." Damn. Heat burst across Charlie's skin. That look was so hot.

"I'll take that as a promise."

"Good. Now get up and get dressed. Quick." The urgency in Elle's voice made Charlie want to go slowly, but this wasn't her house and she didn't want to be a bad guest for Reiko and Yolande, who'd been so incredible these last few days. Surely this Tom Scottridge nonsense would die down soon. Some other scandal would get the media's attention and she'd be forgotten. At least until her mum's fucking movie was released.

She fought the instinct to tease Elle and jumped off the couch instead. The sharp intake of Elle's breath made her smile and she couldn't help it. Charlie strutted across the room. Naked apart from her bra. She brushed past Elle and delighted in the way Elle stroked down her spine and squeezed her butt. Nice.

Gooseflesh painted her skin, and it had nothing to do with the air temperature. Sadly, her display was short lived as she stepped into the guest bedroom and closed the door. She sat heavily on the bed as doubt suddenly rushed around her body like a dark cloud. What would happen once she was dressed? She'd never spent time with Elle afterwards. Elle usually left. Would she leave now? And why didn't Charlie want her to? She threw on some clothes, quickly, so she could rush back into the main living space of Yolande and Reiko's amazing apartment and talk to Elle before she left. Could she convince Elle to stay for dinner? Would Elle want to stay? Was Charlie worth it? Ergh, that anxious thought could fuck off. Of course she was worth it. Whether Elle stayed or not had zero to do with Charlie's self-worth. She threw open the door and sighed. Elle was seated in a chair, her head bent over her phone screen.

"It's true, you know." Charlie hadn't told anyone else, not even her friends who had offered her a place to stay.

"What is?"

"Tom Scottridge is my dad." She stared out the window at the Thames. As usual, it was a muddy brown colour and only the architecture of London made it beautiful.

Elle stood up and slipped her phone into the back pocket of her jeans. She tilted her head, staring at Charlie until she wanted to hide behind her hands.

"Don't look at me like that. I'm still the same person. It doesn't matter who my dad is."

Elle's mouth tightened with the corners pointed downwards. "Sorry."

"Mum only told me last week," Charlie answered the question that Elle didn't ask. "I grew up fatherless. I always figured that Mum had had an affair with someone, or went to a sperm bank, or something, but if she didn't want to talk about it, then neither would I. It didn't really matter." Charlie had been content, growing up on a soap opera set, doing her homework in her mum's cabin while she finished working for the day, then they'd go home together on the tube to their apartment.

Elle almost nodded. "And now everyone knows."

Charlie laughed bitterly. "No. Now everyone thinks they know. Tom Scottridge's PR team have been silent, and Mum sent me a rude text for calling the press on her." That had pissed Charlie off and she hadn't figured out how to respond just yet. The longer she put it off, the more it looked like her mum was correct. On the other hand, Charlie didn't want to throw more fuel on that particular fire.

"What?"

"She's just covering her arse. If she blames me, then she hasn't breached her non-disclosure contract." Charlie suddenly knew what to do. She grabbed her phone from the table and sent her mother a quick reply: *Wasn't me.*

"Her what?" Elle's confusion reminded Charlie of herself when she'd first heard of her mum's agreement with bloody Tom Scottridge. He hadn't even been that famous when Charlie had been conceived; what an arrogant fuck he must be to insist on such a thing! Couldn't possibly have a baby inconveniencing his future career.

Charlie rolled her eyes. "Apparently she signed a non-disclosure agreement with Tom Scottridge. If she doesn't tell anyone that I'm his daughter, then she gets a monthly payment from him for my care."

"But you are all grown up now?"

Charlie sat heavily on the couch. "Oh. I am. Do you think…"

No, she couldn't have… Could her mother have leaked the information on purpose? Yes, she would do that. Charlie had even assumed that was why Mum had decided to come to Seraph's with Tom that night, because she wanted people to see the three of them together and jump to conclusions. Not that Charlie looked anything like Tom with his sharp blue eyes and chiselled jaw and … yeah, the same colour hair as her. Well, that meant nothing and she usually wore a wig when she was on stage. That night, she'd MC'ed wearing a bright red 1920s bob cut wig and a matching flapper dress covered in sequins. She'd looked amazing and her social media had responded well, even before the news had come out. Since then, she hadn't wanted to look at her socials. Her notifications were probably out of control. There was no *probably* about it; she'd seen some of them when she'd picked up her phone to reply to Mum. She put her phone back on the table with the screen facing downwards so she didn't have to see.

"I don't know. What do you think?" Elle asked.

"I think the movie business can be brutal and actors will do anything to get press." Charlie didn't blame her mum for taking advantage of this situation for the sake of her career, but she wouldn't have minded a bit of a warning from her. She didn't appreciate being toyed with for the sake of someone else's career.

"Hey, are you guys decent?" Yolande's voice rang out from the hallway.

"Yes. Come in." Charlie glanced at Elle, whose cheeks glowed pink. She winked at her, and the colour deepened, making her brown eyes look shinier and wider.

"I'd better go."

Charlie shook her head. "Stay for dinner. Please." She had nothing else to do and an evening spent chatting with Elle, Reiko, and Yolande sounded brilliant.

"Sorry, I can't." Elle didn't explain further, just walked to the door, and spoke quietly to Charlie's friends as she slipped on her sandals and left.

Charlie squared her shoulders; well, she didn't need to get to know her hook ups. Her body was sated and now she could hang with real friends, people who stuck around for her and gave her a safe place to stay when she needed it. Elle was merely a distraction … A wonderful physical distraction that Charlie wanted to know better. It was obvious that Elle didn't want the same thing; she'd played with her toy and then left. Charlie chuckled bitterly. She'd done that to so many people over the years, before the pandemic, so maybe this was just karma coming to bite her on the arse.

"Are you coming to work with us tonight? Reiko will order a ride share, so no one will see you." Yolande waltzed into the room and Charlie swallowed. She'd forgotten that everyone else had to work.

"May as well." She shrugged. What else was she going to do? Hang out by herself again while feeling sorry for herself? Nah. She'd brave the press and go to work. Why should her mum's nonsense stop her doing what she loved?

8

_____

Elle was glad she'd taken the train to Joey's birthday party because after a day spent with her family, with all of them gushing over her very cute nephew, she was done. She didn't mind the gushing. Joey was very cute and she loved seeing him. It was the not-so-subtle backhanders about her age and singleness that hurt. If they were waiting for her to be a dutiful daughter and marry some white cishet man who would sell her business so she would have time to dedicate to his children, then they'd be waiting for fucking ever.

She made her excuses—she had too much work on—and left as soon as was polite so she didn't have to get a ride home in Hugh's car with Willow and Joey. It'd been days since she'd last seen Charlie and she couldn't let go of the disappointed expression that had covered Charlie's face when Elle had walked away.

Today's party had been the perfect reminder for how much she needed to keep her business flourishing. She needed to pay her parents back quickly. They hadn't asked about the money.

They'd never be so obvious. Instead displayed their disapproval in other ways, like when they'd asked after her ex, Campbell, 'What a nice boy he was, blah blah', as they conveniently forgot that he'd dumped her just before Christmas because he hadn't wanted to go to their family dinner. They hadn't cared when he'd been rude about her weight at various family events —why would they? They agreed with him.

And apparently a little thing like a global pandemic shouldn't have stopped her from finding a nice man to marry. If not Campbell, then someone else similar. Someone else who would help them keep her contained as they liked. Fucking hell.

She'd rather marry Charlie than some bloke.

No.

Her breath caught in her throat. Charlie was just a hook up; great in bed, the best kisser she'd ever been with, someone who challenged her physically, teased her, and … all of that. She should probably admit to herself that she wasn't going to fuck Charlie out of her system any time soon. They'd been doing this for a couple of years now—apart from the enforced break—and each time only made Elle want to spend more time with Charlie.

Unfortunately it was obvious that Charlie wasn't the marrying type. They'd never been exclusive with each other. Elle knew that she was only one of Charlie's many hook ups, and it didn't use to bother her. Back then, Elle had been on a few dates and some had ended with sex. None of it had mattered; just a bit of fun. Elle had never even given it more than a passing thought until today. Part of the thrill of being with Charlie was knowing that it was temporary, a mutual momentary pleasure without the emotional weight of a relationship. Why did she yearn for more now?

The tube would take her right past the stop for Seraph's before heading through town to her place. It'd be pretty easy to get off and spend the evening at Seraph's before using Charlie to get rid of this pent up frustration caused by her family's expectations of perfection. Whatever she did, it was never enough for her parents. She shook out her hands. Using Charlie like this didn't feel right either. They'd always had a mutual thing; where had this thought come from? Did she really want to use Charlie? No. They might have never defined what they had but thinking about using Charlie for pleasurable gain felt like a gross abuse of their mutual joy. Did she want to share her day with Charlie and have someone listen to her woes? No. Maybe? That sounded a lot like what people who were in a relationship might do. She couldn't quite picture Charlie in that role, as an emotional comfort for her. She blew out a long breath. What she truly needed was to focus on work … except the job with the highest priority on her list was the refit at Seraph's. She thumbed open her phone and scrolled down before dialling Beth.

"Hi."

"Hi Beth. Have you got time this evening for a quick meeting? I know it's not ideal—"

"Yes. I wanted to talk over the plan you sent through. Is it possible for you to come here before opening tonight?" Beth's idea was exactly the excuse Elle needed. It was time to admit it to herself; she wanted to see Charlie and work was a good reason to put herself in the same space as Charlie.

"I'll be there in less than half an hour." Elle almost said she was already on the tube but stopped herself because that made her sound disorganised.

"So soon?"

"Yes. I was going past on the tube and it occurred to me that you might be in tonight." So much for not telling Beth. But her question about timing had opened up the need for an explanation. It didn't matter why she was on the tube or where she was going. *Shut up, brain. Just go to focus and get to work.* After a day with her family, she usually needed some time to unscramble and decompress. Heading into Seraph's for a business meeting was probably not the best choice, but it was too late now.

"Brilliant. I'll see you soon."

Elle stood up and waited by the door. She really needed to clear her head and a walk usually helped. Getting out here, a couple of stops early, would give her the walk she needed. There was something about walking that helped her creatively, and hopefully striding out through London's busy streets would help stretch her brain and figure out the puzzle that was the layout at Seraph's. Something wasn't quite right with her plans and it kept niggling at her, like a seed in her sock. Behind the stage needed to be streamlined and made more practical, in a cost-effective way that meant the least amount of structural changes.

Summer evenings in London weren't meant for furious walking, so by the time Elle arrived at Seraph's, her shirt stuck to her skin and her thighs had rubbed together uncomfortably against her pants. She needed a shower. The best she could do was grab the front of her shirt and shake it to get some air against her skin. Hopefully her deodorant would work well and she wouldn't stink too much for this meeting.

"Elle. Beth told me you'd be here." Walter opened the front door and waved her through.

She thanked him as she headed inside. All the lights were on in the bar area as several of the staff got it ready for tonight's show. The bright lights illuminated how tired and old all the décor was. If Elle had a bigger budget for this refit, she'd strip everything out and replace it all, but she'd have to make do with a more cost-effective makeover. With the right lighting, people wouldn't notice the way the wood on the tables had been cleaned too many times. Redoing the varnish might fix the tables and make them look new again, but there was no way to hide the way the chairs were so tired looking. They were all metal and wood so there was a chance that a paint job might help; although it wasn't usually cost effective to repaint furniture given the amount of labour involved in the preparation phase. She could take one with her to her next upholstery class and figure out the best way to refresh it.

A change to the layout would make the biggest difference to the appearance of the place. A couple of plants at the ends of the bar, new lighting, and changing the table locations to make a better flow for patrons and staff. The edge of the stage was going to look amazing when she added a new façade to it, something a bit more hardwearing than the current chipped and dented old wood panelling. Perhaps corrugated iron—no, too industrial—maybe slick angled tiles. Not subway tiles, they were so 2000s … something similar but in a herringbone pattern perhaps.

"Elle." Beth waved at her from a door beside the stage.

"Hi." Whatever she put along the edge of the stage needed

to fade into the background lighting and not dominate the space. That was the problem with tiles, they were too shiny, she needed something more matt in texture, like a pale wood. Yeah. Beth laid the printed out plans on one of the tables and beckoned her over.

"I'm glad you have these. I just came from my nephew's birthday party and I was going right past so I didn't have them with me." Elle cringed. She sounded so disorganised, nothing like the successful business owner that she wanted to be.

"Happy birthday to your nephew."

"Thanks. What do you think of them?" Elle waved at the plan.

"They seem okay."

"But?" Elle waited for the question from Beth.

"I'm struggling to picture what it'll look like." Beth swept her hand over the plans and Elle suddenly understood. When people without architectural training looked at plans, they often found it difficult to imagine the plans in three dimensional space.

"I can make up a model if you think it would be easier than a flat plan?"

Beth raised one eyebrow. "Wouldn't that cost extra?"

"Usually. I'll do this one on the house because I've enjoyed many evenings at Seraph's."

Beth frowned. "No. I can't let you do that. I know what it takes to run a business, and you'll never succeed if you do work for free." After a whole day with her family who criticised every tiny thing she did, Beth's comment sent a cold chill across Elle's neck. She should've framed the offer differently, and even thinking about how she could have done something to change the outcome pinched at her awkwardly. Old habits died hard, or in her case, didn't die at all.

"It's not for free if it means my client understands the scope of work better and can make necessary adjustments before we start construction."

"You just said it would be free."

Elle breathed in and out slowly. "Think of it as a loss leader. I'd rather create a model at this stage than begin building and then have you realise that the space isn't quite what you wanted."

"Okay." Beth frowned. "One thing."

"Yes?"

"Do you do this for all your clients?"

Elle fought to maintain a poker face as Beth continued the theme of the day—tell Elle what she was doing wrong—then she nodded slowly. "Typically only for bigger jobs. The refit at Seraph's is quite complex though, so it would be worth a three dimensional model to ensure we are all agreed before commencing work."

"Okay."

"Hey, are these the plans you've been making?" Charlie asked. Where had she arrived from? Elle had been so focused on convincing Beth that she wasn't a fuck up that she hadn't seen Charlie walk into the room.

"Yes."

Charlie leaned over the table and traced her finger along the plan. "So this is the stage? And the bar? And what's this?"

Elle tried to breathe normally, except she swore she could feel Charlie's finger on her skin, burning a pathway, instead of pointing to the plan. She swallowed. "Um, that's the new dance studio room. I expanded it, because the wall on this side isn't a structural wall, so we can take it out and join it up with this tiny cupboard. Then over here, I've widened the ramp onto the stage…"

"You remembered."

"What? Oh, yes, you said that you and the other dancers found the current one too narrow for some of the costumes. I've widened it out so the car will fit up it, which should be plenty of space."

"Should be."

"To do that, I've had to get rid of a few of the smaller storage rooms…"

"Cupboards." Charlie laughed.

Elle tried not to argue. "Yes. And I've juggled some of the other spaces to create a larger costume store room, and a cleaners room, as well as swapping Beth's office with one of the change rooms to utilise the space better." She pointed to the sections of the plan as she went and when her finger touched Charlie's hand, she tried not to jerk hers away at the electric contact. "If it makes no sense, don't worry. I'm going to make a 3D model so you can walk a Lego figure through it. It usually helps people visualise the spaces when they have a small version of it."

"Cool."

"Don't you have somewhere to be?" Beth's cool question hovered awkwardly. Charlie straightened up.

"Of course. No press yet?"

"No." Beth smiled. "It's been really busy since you've been splashed all over the news. Maybe we should invent a different dad for you next week."

"Hey!" Charlie laughed and the joyful sound bounced

around the empty bar. "You'll have to pay me a bonus for marketing the hell out of this place."

Beth winked at her. "Good luck. Go on, let's get this show on the road and I can talk business with my designer."

"So fancy. Imagine." Charlie gave Beth a friendly kiss on the cheek and walked off. Once she was a few steps away, she looked back over her shoulder and winked at Elle.

Heat bloomed. Elle's shirt was already hot and sticky from her walk here and now she wanted to pull it away from her skin. Again.

"Don't mind Charlie. She's brash and cocky but she's the best damned MC I've ever had."

Elle cleared her throat. "It's fine."

Beth sent her a quizzical look and then her eyes widened slowly. "I can't believe it's taken me so long to place you. You used to come here quite often before…"

"Yes."

Beth smiled. "Why didn't you say something?"

Elle shrugged. "I'm here for work. Obviously I'm grateful for the recommendation from Reiko for my business and I didn't want to complicate things by mentioning that I used to be a regular here."

"It's a shame. I've been trying to work out where I knew you from for ages."

"I'm sure all the faces blur together after a while."

"A little, but I pride myself on knowing all our regulars. And… You used to sit at the end of the bar and chat with Charlie afterwards. She didn't tell me she knew you."

Elle's cheeks grew warm and she hoped her blush wasn't too apparent. "I can't comment on what Charlie choses to share with her boss."

Beth laughed. "Oh fuck. You've slept with her, haven't you?"

Elle lifted her chin higher. "I hope you won't judge me poorly for…"

"—being young and having a healthy sex life with one of my hottest employees? Hell no. Good for you." Beth's laughter rang louder, echoing around the empty room.

"Um, thanks."

"It's only awkward if we make it like that, and it seems like you and Charlie get along well enough when you aren't fucking."

OMG, had Beth really said that? Elle's face flamed hot. "Yeah." What else could she say?

"Then we don't have a problem here, do we?"

"No. I'm good, as long as you are. I mean, it's a bit of a unique situation for me at work."

"You've never fucked a client's employee before?" The teasing glint in Beth's eyes made Elle laugh.

"Stop."

"Sorry. I should be teasing Charlie, not you. I hope you aren't uncomfortable."

Elle shook her head. "No. I mean, it's not a topic that has ever come up in work meetings before now, but I guess it's okay in this circumstance. You probably have a right to know about stuff involving your staff." She wasn't going to call it a relationship; that wasn't quite what her and Charlie had.

"Make sure you invite me to the wedding."

"What? It's not…"

Beth laughed again. "I'm teasing. It's what we do at Seraph's. You'll have to get used to it if you are going to be working with us all for a while."

Elle tried to nod solemnly even though she was out of her depth here. "Okay." She would've folded up the plan and moved on, but it was Beth's copy. "Shall we talk about the options for the stage area?" She opened the files using a cloud app on her phone, so she could show Beth some of the options she'd been putting together. Anything was better than Beth teasing her about Charlie.

9

_____

Charlie leaned against the bloody Mini. She was a coward. Seeing Elle reminded her of the fucking amazing sex they'd had the other day, the way Elle had teased her, and soothed her, and helped her get rid of all the pent-up energy caused by her mother's media dramas. All of that would be fine, until she'd walked closer and started to tease her and then it had all come rushing back.

Every time they fucked, Elle made an excuse afterwards and left. And now instead of talking to her about it, Charlie was hanging out next to a bloody car, too timid to ask Elle why. Why didn't Elle stick around for her? Before … it hadn't mattered. Charlie had been the one to leave, or at least when Elle left, Charlie had been relieved that she hadn't wanted a relationship. Now … when Charlie tried to relive her old life it didn't satisfy her. She wanted more. She wanted people to stick around for her, to want to be with her for more than just an opportunity to further their career, or just as a good fuck sometimes.

Charlie was just like the Mini. A pretty shell with no substance inside. The car didn't even have an engine. It was just the outside skin of a car that they used as a prop sometimes, just as she was a prop for all her hook ups. Not that she'd been with many of them since Elle had walked back into her life. Hmm, she squeezed her eyes shut, trying to push away that realisation. She wasn't going to think about why she'd almost been exclusive with Elle.

Had she really? She opened her eyes and stared at the bloody car.

She'd much rather think about the car, than contemplate why she was unsatisfied with everyone except Elle. Ben had rigged up a pulley system and a ramp, so they could pull it onto the stage and then roll it back off whenever they wanted. It was all his fault. The first night he had worked here as a brand new technician, Yolande had walked out on stage to do her 1950s showgirl routine and he'd muttered something about how much cooler it would be if she had a car from the same era. Charlie had shoved him on the shoulder and told him not to be silly. How could they possibly get a car on stage? And he'd proved her wrong. She couldn't even be mad because it was the coolest fucking thing.

"Which wall do you want to move?" Beth's voice carried across the room and for a second, Charlie contemplated hiding inside the Mini as Elle walked in with Beth. Coward.

"This one." Elle walked over to the far wall, and Charlie was amused to see her glance sideways at her, then focus on her work. "If we remove it, we can widen the ramp on the other side of the wall, and this room also becomes a lot bigger. Then we'd build shelving all along that wall, and—" Elle waved around the room, "then the whole room will be more functional as a stage prop room."

"I like it. At the moment our props and costumes are stored all over the place but having next to the stage would make a lot more sense."

"Yes. I had a good talk to Ben about stage movements and other technical stuff as part of my planning process."

"Ben is great." Charlie couldn't help herself, jumping into the conversation when she was clearly not required. "He designed the system to get the car on and off the stage."

"Yes, he showed it to me, and we've included that in the final design as well as additional space for his sound system."

"No more tripping over cables?" Charlie could only hope. Whenever they had someone new come and dance, she had to walk them through the whole back stage and make sure they weren't going to injure themselves on all the different things lying around the place.

"Yes. Ben has helped me work out a plan that will ensure a much neater space back stage with more room in the wings for dancers and their costumes as well as a better space for the sound equipment. Not much needed changing, to be honest."

Charlie couldn't decide if Elle was being rude or not. "I'm sure we could've worked that out ourselves."

"Charlie. You know that Ben has done the best he can with no budget. These changes come at some considerable cost, and we should listen to Elle's expertise." Beth scolded Charlie and she nodded, rather than roll her eyes, because she knew she was being a bit of a bitch. It was her natural defence mechanism.

"Okay."

"Don't stress about the money, Charlie. Just keep putting

together amazing on stage programs. Between the COVID grant money, and the public's need to get out of their houses, we are doing well. Having Tom Scottridge and your Mum here last week helped a ton as well." Beth was so pragmatic, and it helped settle the churning in Charlie's stomach. Her shoulders relaxed a little. She'd learned about the grant money recently but had forgotten until Beth mentioned it again just now.

"Cool. Well, Elle, if there is anything you need, just let me know." Charlie turned to leave.

"There is one thing." At Elle's voice, Charlie paused and slowly turned back towards her and Beth.

"Yeah?"

"Can we chat once I'm done here?"

Beth laughed. "You two love birds can talk now if you want. I'm out of here." She paced out of the room, and the door slammed extra loudly as a final parting message.

"What was that about?" Charlie puzzled at her boss's cryptic comment. "Love birds?"

Elle's face was bright red. "She recognised me from before."

"Oh." Trust her boss to finally recognise Elle as one of her hook ups at the most inconvenient time.

"It's not a problem. We talked about it and she made fun of me."

"She would. Okay, cool. Hey, can I ask you a question?" Charlie couldn't contain her curiosity anymore. She needed to know if Elle really only wanted sex or if she might be open to more. There was something interesting about her and Charlie wanted to get to know her better. Rather than hide here—so unlike her—she made the sudden decision to be bold and have a crack at something more. But Elle's phone rang.

"Sorry, can it wait? I need to get this."

"Sure." What else could she say? Technically Elle was here to work, it made sense to prioritise that over Charlie's uncertainty. She hated this doubt that had arrived at some point during the lockdowns and wouldn't go away. Maybe a change —like a proper relationship—might be what she needed to find herself again. It made no sense, but at this point, Charlie was keen to try anything to regain her the thrill she used to get from burlesque.

"Hugh. What's the matter? … Yeah, sure, ask away."

Why did this Hugh get to ask a question and she didn't? Charlie wanted to give this guy the finger as he got priority over her. She gulped at the way her heart fluttered and her blood pounded in her veins. What did that mean? Nothing. Probably nothing.

"Willow did nothing wrong. I like her. … Yeah, she's really lovely, Hugh. … I wasn't lying, I had work to do. I'm literally in a work meeting right now. … Yeah. I know I said that, but … Hugh, please believe me. I wouldn't say anything I don't mean. … It's not Willow." Elle was working hard to convince Hugh that she liked Willow, whoever that was. "Yes, let's have dinner soon. I'd like that. … Hey, it's going to be okay. Willow is really good for you, and I'll always like her for the way she's so honest and open with you. It's obvious that she understands our situation and she does her best. … I know. It's fine. … Okay, I'll look at my calendar and work out a date. … Bye."

Charlie shouldn't ask—it was none of her business who these people were in Elle's life—so she fell back on an old trick and made a joke instead. "Your situation? Are you in a poly relationship with Hugh and Willow? Can I join in?"

Elle's eyes widened until they were huge in her face. She shook her head so hard that strands of black hair flew out of her ponytail and dangled enticingly around her face. "What? How does your brain go there?"

"Well?"

"Hugh is my brother. Willow is his wife."

"Oh. Well, that's boring compared to what I was thinking." Charlie winked.

Elle put her phone in her pocket and rubbed her cheeks. "I shouldn't ask, but have you ever?"

"Had a trio? A couple of times. It can be fun with the right people."

"Don't your limbs get all tangled up?"

Charlie burst out laughing. Not just at the innocent question but also at the look on Elle's face; something like confusion and curiosity all mixed up with a wide naïve stare.

"Well?"

"No. I mean, sometimes, if that's what people want, but it's just sex and fun."

Elle nodded. "Okay."

"Fine. I'll bite. Why does your brother think you don't like his wife?"

Elle stiffened. "I do like Willow. She's very kind and simple and exactly what he needs."

"Simple?" Charlie couldn't believe Elle had said that. Didn't she realise it was an insult?

"Oh God, no. I meant that she's honest and kind and doesn't manipulate him and that type of open simplicity is what Hugh needs in a relationship. Someone who is exactly what they say they are."

"Understood." Charlie needed to stop with the questions, but she couldn't. "So why does your brother need someone who won't manipulate him?"

Elle sagged, and Charlie rushed towards her in case she fainted. She needn't have bothered as Elle stiffened again.

"Hugh had a rough upbringing. My parents have certain expectations for us, and more so for him because he's the oldest son. If you asked anyone in our village, they'd say that we were the perfect family, but it's all fake. My parents do a lot of, um … work to ensure everyone knows how perfect we are."

Charlie nodded. "So I take it they don't know you are queer?"

Elle bowed her head. "Hell no. And even if they did know, they'd just pretend—"

"—that you don't exist?"

The sigh from Elle filled the room with its volume. "I don't think I want to find out."

"Why don't you walk away? Make your own family. Blood doesn't make a family." And didn't Charlie know that. Fucking Tom Scottridge was her biological father and he'd paid Mum to keep quiet about it for all of her twenty-eight years. Great actor. Shitty father. She swallowed back a growl; at least he'd paid. Did that count for something? She didn't know. The idea that she was some famous cishet white guy's dirty secret was really fucking gross.

"You don't have to look so disgusted."

Charlie took a second to force her face into what she hoped was a more neutral expression. "Sorry, I was thinking of my own family and their mess. That's how I know that you can create your own family and you don't have to put up with people's crap just because you have a genetic connection."

"It's not that easy."

Charlie raised her eyebrows.

"Fine. I would walk away…" Elle sighed again. Her gaze darted around the room, as if she was trying to figure out which reasons she wanted to share. "…except Hugh wants to keep a relationship with them. He…" If Elle wanted to blame her brother, it was none of Charlie's business.

"Why does he want a relationship with people who seem to be okay with letting him believe his wife doesn't like his sister?" Charlie probably had that tangled up. The whole thing sounded pretty fucking messy. At the very least, Elle's parents didn't sound very kind.

"We've been taught all our lives about keeping up appearances, and he doesn't want to be the one who ruins the perfect family. For all our parent's sins, it would break their hearts if we stopped trying."

"Would it? Or would it just break their perfect little fake existence?"

Elle frowned. If her brown eyes held bullets, Charlie would be riddled with them by now. "It's not your business how I choose to deal with my parents. They've never beaten us or abused us."

Charlie blinked slowly, and her chest felt hollow as Elle used the lowest bar possible to discuss her parents. Charlie's mum might be a self-absorbed actress and she might occasionally ask Charlie why she wasn't using her talents in the same field, but she cared for Charlie and supported her even when she didn't understand why Charlie did burlesque instead of acting.

For Charlie, there wasn't much difference between the two creative forms of expression. Great burlesque dancers were brilliant actors, and besides, her job was more than just the dancing. She loved teaching classes. She adored organising each evening's event, especially as she got sneak previews of all the new talent. She had a slightly tense relationship with her mother merely because she was, well, herself, but Charlie would never stoop to saying something as wild as implying her mum was a good person because she'd never abused her. What? Make it make sense. Elle's parents must be complete shitheads if that was the benchmark she used to excuse their behaviour.

Elle stood with her hands on her hips, still glaring at Charlie, as if this discussion was her fault and not the fault of Elle's shitty parents. "So what if they have high standards for us, that's not enough to throw away a whole relationship."

"Okay," Charlie whispered. If she let the urge to keep asking questions take over, Elle was going to blow this up into a big fight, and Charlie wanted to avoid that. "All families are kind of fucked up, so you just keep doing what you think is best."

"What does that mean?"

Charlie held up her hands. "No judgement. Fuck. My mum just threw me to the paparazzi to get more press for her career. I have some idea about how family can be selfish." There was nothing like a bit of media focus and a week away from work to give her too much time to think about whether her entire existence was shallow and pointless. She loved burlesque. There was just one problem. Ever since she'd been locked down away from her audience, she'd had too much time to contemplate who she was without people cheering for her. And the answers she'd found so far did her no credit. She was empty and shallow.

Elle's mouth twitched at the corners, almost into the beginnings of a grin. "Fair enough. Are you okay?"

"Yeah."

"Are you sure?" All the fury had left Elle's voice. Charlie was left with two options: walk away before she admitted some of her real feelings to Elle, or kiss her as a distraction. There really only was one option. She strode towards Elle and wrapped her hands around her head.

"I'm fine." Charlie leaned down and kissed Elle, who responded immediately.

They fell into their usual dance, with Elle stretching up on the tips of her toes as she pressed her body against Charlie. Charlie stroked her tongue deep into Elle's mouth, savouring her taste, with an extra hint of salt today. The beautiful softness of her lips as they moved against hers. Every time they kissed, Elle would demand more. She'd control the pace and depth of their kiss, and Charlie let her because there was something incredible about the way Elle grew in confidence through their kisses. The hesitance she often showed when they talked disappeared as she stroked her hands down Charlie's spine and gripped her arse with firm fingers. Their height difference only enhanced the way Elle took over the dance of their mouths. Each touch from Elle sent heat spiralling along her skin, burning through her veins, until she wanted more. She wanted to be bent over the bonnet of the car and fucked with a strap on, or have Elle's mouth on her. She shuddered. Not today.

"I've got my period." Charlie hated to put a stop to this

kiss but from the way Elle's hands were exploring, she'd get a bit of a surprise soon, and that wasn't very cool at all.

"Oh."

"We can still kiss."

Elle slid her hands up to Charlie's waist. "We certainly can. You are very accomplished as a kisser."

"Why thank you." Charlie would've bowed except her body was pressed up against Elle, so she winked instead. For some unknown reason, the wink felt wrong, like she was faking it. Instead of bending to kiss Elle again, she pulled her closer into a hug and nuzzled her face against Elle's neck. She was so soft and smooth, and her skin smelled like salt and fabric softener and her very own perfume with a hint of florals.

Elle ran one hand up Charlie's spine until she cupped the back of Charlie's head. "It's going to be okay."

Charlie didn't need to ask. "I know. It was just my mum making the best of her career. It's not easy being an actress on a show like Chelsea Avenue. Characters get written out for the most minor reasons, and to have an opportunity to act alongside a high profile actor is something she needs to make the most of."

"Even if it meant hurting you?" Elle's whisper was a soft breeze against her ear.

"She didn't hurt me. She just caused a temporary interruption to my life."

Elle brushed her thumb back and forth over Charlie's neck and Charlie wished they could lie in bed together and soothe each other so gently. She almost jerked away; since when did she want to be cuddled? What was wrong with her?

"This has been nice and everything, but I'd better get back

to work." She pushed away from Elle and walked away without a backward glance. All that talk of Elle's crappy parents had left her feeling sympathetic or something, and she'd bloody spoken about her own stuff. She never shared with her hook ups. Mixing sex and friendship and emotions was a path to misery. Thinking about asking Elle to be exclusive with her was an aberration. She ought to follow her mum's example and keep friendship and sex separate. Life was much less messy that way.

10

Today was the big day. The sun was barely up when she'd left the house this morning and now Elle stood outside the front door at Seraph's, waiting for Walter to let her in as they'd arranged. She hadn't seen Charlie since they'd kissed desperately a couple of weeks ago. Maybe it was for the best; having Charlie leave first was odd and Elle had tried not to dwell on it. She'd failed of course because nothing about the way they were interacting at the moment was the same as before. Maybe they weren't compatible when they weren't fucking each other senseless? Elle wanted to bury her face in her hands; how had it come to this? She wanted Charlie for more than sex, wanted to get to know her, wanted to hug her when she was upset, wanted to be the one Charlie sheltered with when her mother, bloody Lottie Alcott-James, was in the media and the paparazzi wanted a piece of Charlie.

Elle's phone dinged with an incoming message.

Beth: What time did you say the builders were turning up?

Elle: 8am

Beth: Fuck. So early! Walter will let them in.

Elle: They wanted to start at 6.

Beth: Ergh. We close only a few hours before that.

The plans for Seraph's had been approved, not just by Beth, but by all the relevant authorities. A text from Beth yesterday had confirmed the grant money had arrived, and the building contractors were going to start today. Technically, Elle didn't need to oversee the works, but this was her first non-residential project, which was a much better reason to head into Seraph's than submitting to an irrational need to see Charlie. Every day, she'd written a quick text to say hi and then deleted it, because what would she say next? Sorry for finding it easier to argue with you than stand up to my parents?

Elle: I know. That's why I negotiated a later start time.

Since starting this project, she'd spent more time talking to Charlie than ever before, and Elle wanted more than the little glimpses that Charlie showed her. The problem with wanting such a thing was that she would have to become more open with Charlie too, and that whole discussion about her parents had pissed her off no end. It hadn't been until she'd been chatting to Willow the next day that she realised why.

Charlie had skirted far too close to the truth when she'd mentioned that Elle didn't have to succumb to her parent's demands. Of course, Elle couldn't walk away just yet; she still owed a debt to her parents for D&Y Designs. They'd wanted her to name her business after them; Denbigh And Yadav Designs. It was bad enough that her parents had saddled her with a double-barrelled name. She'd protested, saying that it wasn't worth the risk to the family name if the business failed. Businesses failed all the time for all sorts of reasons, and it was only sensible to plan for such a thing. When her parents had threatened to withdraw the loan over the name, she'd almost walked away. Had she really been willing to wait another three years in her boring job doing the filing for Blessings Office Furniture? No. She couldn't waste her life any longer, so she'd found a name that satisfied them without being about them and taken the loan. One day, she'd figure out an alternative for D&Y, and until then, she'd have to deal with her parents taking all the credit for her success and nearly having naming rights. She almost had the loan paid off. Soon, she might be able to face a future where she could be brave and maybe… just maybe, listen to Charlie's advice. She knew her parent's demands weren't rational, it wasn't what loving parents did for their children. Loving parents would help without such egotistic conditions. Wouldn't they?

The door opened and a blurry eyed Walter stood inside wearing a pink dressing gown that barely covered anything.

"Good morning." Elle spluttered at the unexpected sight of all that brown skin and tattoo covered masculine muscles. Fucking hell. A thin strand of pink satin tied around Walter's waist was the only thing keeping the gown together and covering his… um… She dared not look lower, even though her cheeks were blazing hot. How embarrassing. He must know she was blushing at the sight of him.

"Come in. I'm going back to bed." He walked off and Elle caught an accidental glimpse of his arse. His thighs were covered in impressive tattoos, and she closed her eyes for a while. It wouldn't do to be caught staring at a married man. She didn't feel the pull of lust or attraction, only bemusement at his choice of gown, and admiration for the confident way he didn't seem to care what anyone thought of him.

The flutter in her chest came and went. Was everyone who

worked at Seraph's so confident in their own skin? She couldn't imagine what that would be like. Imagine just being comfortable enough to walk around virtually naked and not caring who saw? She'd only felt like that once. With Charlie, here behind the stage in one of the many hallways, when she'd pulled down her pants and enjoyed the way Charlie licked her, kneading her arse with those long elegant fingers, until she'd come. She shivered. Coming here was a mistake.

With a deep breath, she pushed away all those pesky feelings and stepped inside. This was work; she needed to make this job a success to pay off her debt. She closed the front door, then walked through Seraph's checking that everything was ready for today's demolition. The builders were due in five minutes at the back door, so she made her way there. As she went past Charlie's office, a soft murmur filled the air and she peeked into the room. Charlie was fast asleep in her chair with a blanket wrapped around her. She couldn't possibly be comfortable, sleeping like that. Elle coughed and Charlie cracked open one eye.

"Hey."

"Good morning, Charlie. Should you be sleeping like that?"

"I'm fine." Charlie stood up—an elegant motion like a dancer arising from a tucked position into a tall stance—and the blanket fell to the ground, exposing a lot of bare skin. In less than a minute, Elle had seen more naked flesh than she had in months. Charlie was so incredibly gorgeous—standing there in the remnants of last night's outfit—far more impressive than Walter's muscular tattooed thighs, and the odd comparison sent a blast of radiant heat across Elle's skin. She gulped.

"Um…"

"I hope you brought coffee?" Just like Walter, Charlie didn't care about who saw her body. Elle could only dream of having that level of confidence.

"No, but once I let the builders in, I can grab us some from across the road."

"Great. Hold on, did you say builders?"

"Yes. They start the demolition today."

Charlie growled under the breath and grabbed the blanket. "Shit. I don't usually sleep here but last night sucked. Beth was pacing around the place and everyone was on edge. Poor Reiko dropped a whole case of vodka bottles and glass went everywhere."

"Oh no."

"Yeah, basically a shit night, and I ended up working extra hours to help clean up and stuff. I thought I'd grab a quick sleep here before going home."

Elle nodded. "Beth was probably nervous about today. It's going to be alright. Maybe you should go home and get some proper sleep."

"Yeah, probably, but then I'll miss all the fun." Charlie threw the blanket on her chair and started putting on some clothes. There was a loud banging on the back door and Elle dragged in a deep breath.

"That'll be the builders." She marched down the narrow hallway to the back door and opened it, expecting to see the foreman, Siddarth, not … him. Campbell, her ex. Her stomach dropped; he was the last person she wanted to deal with today.

"Hi Elle."

Like a fool, she said, "Hi."

"Life has really gone downhill for you. You're a slutty dancer now, really? Good thing I dumped your fat arse." Campbell instantly proved why she'd been so pathetic to stay with him. He used to say mean stuff like that all the time and she'd let him because … Well, because her parents had trained her to put up with insults. No more.

"Fuck off, Campbell. Where is Siddarth?"

"He'll be here soon."

"Good. Then I can get him to fire your lazy arse." Elle hadn't needed the reminder for why she'd dodged a bullet when he'd dumped her. Why had she put up with that crap? Why hadn't she dumped him? She'd given him all her time and been grateful for every scrap of attention he paid her. Fuck, she'd been so desperate and unhappy. He wasn't even that cute, not with that mean sneer on his face.

"You are in charge here? Nah. Move out of the way. Let us in."

Elle glared at him, determined never to be so pathetic again. "No. You'll have to wait for your boss." She closed the door quickly before Campbell had time to react. A long time ago, he'd taken advantage of her lack of confidence. Never again. She might not have the same level of cockiness that Walter, Charlie, and everyone who worked here had, but she owned her own business now. She wasn't going to let a shit-head like Campbell trample over here again. She had some pride now.

"What the fuck was that?"

"My ex being a toad." Elle's neck prickled. "That was so embarrassing. Ergh, what did I ever see in him?"

Charlie laughed. "Everyone has a few regrets in their past."

"Do you?" Elle shouldn't be curious. Surely Charlie

didn't have a regret as awful as Campbell, although she really hoped so. Not for Charlie's sake, but just so she didn't have to feel so … alone and miserable as she confronted her terrible ex.

"There was the sword swallower at the Edinburgh Festival. What the fuck was I thinking? Just because a bloke can shove a long metal thing down his throat doesn't mean he has any other skills. And then there was the time in Paris after the neo-burlesque contest … Fuck, that must be nearly eight years ago now. I managed to break my arm trying to have sex on a trapeze." Charlie rolled up the sleeve of her shirt. "See, I still have a scar."

"Lucky you didn't fall on your head." Elle's mouth seemed determined to say daft things and she wanted to sink under the floor and disappear. What she'd actually wanted to say was something sympathetic, except that would have told Charlie how much she was starting to care for her, and given their last conversation, that was probably the last thing Charlie wanted to hear. Was admiration for Charlie's confidence the same thing as maybe, probably, falling in love with her? No, it couldn't be that.

"What do I do about him?" Once more, Elle proved to the world—to Charlie—how she couldn't deal with conflict. This was her work, her own business, surely she could figure out what to do about a small hiccup. Having Campbell here might feel like a disaster. It didn't have to be. She squared her shoulders in an attempt to ready herself to open the door and sort it out herself.

"I'll get Walter. Sometimes having a huge bloke around is useful." Charlie's solution was better. Having backup would bolster her fragile bravado. "Then you can make him work."

"That's a good plan." By the time she'd finished speaking, Charlie was already speaking to Walter on the phone.

"Sweet. He'll be down in a minute or so. I bet that really pissed him off."

"Who?" Elle twisted her hands together to avoid rubbing her face in a dead giveaway of her internal battle to pretend to be cool about this dreadfully embarrassing situation.

"Your ex. You know when you slammed the door in his face."

Elle chuckled. "Yeah. I'm not looking forward to opening it again."

"Which is why we require Walter. Let the strapping big security guy do his job."

"What job do you need me to do?" Walter asked.

"Seriously, you came wearing Steph's dressing gown?" Charlie threw her head back and laughed, and the sound warmed Elle all the way through. Until then, she hadn't realised how cold the conversation with Campbell had made her. "Oh my God, that is absolute gold."

"Who says it's Steph's dressing gown?" Walter raised one eyebrow. "Now what do you need from me?"

Giggles took over and Elle leaned against the wall with her hand clamped over her mouth, unable to breathe at Walter's retort. She was laughing so hard that her belly hurt and she barely heard Charlie tell Walter about Campbell.

"Pull yourself together," Walter threw the command in her direction then opened the door. Campbell charged directly into the wall that was Walter's chest and bounced off again.

"Who are you?"

"Security. Who are you?"

"Campbell Mason. Builder."

Walter nodded. "Elle is in charge of the building works. You'll report to her." He stepped aside and waved Campbell and the two other builders inside. The three men had to turn their shoulders to fit past Walter, and Elle was glad she'd been shocked out of her giggle fit by Walter's command.

"This way." She walked towards the current ramp to the stage and quickly explained the job. Walter, in his tiny pink dressing gown, stood at the side of the room and watched. His presence was enough to ensure the three builders got to work without any commentary. She pulled out her phone and saw a text from Siddarth asking if she wanted coffee.

"Walter, Charlie. Coffee?"

They both responded positively, and she replied to Siddarth with their orders.

Siddarth: Be there soon. I hope the boys were no trouble.

Elle rolled her eyes. That conversation could wait until later.

O ver an hour later, Elle wanted to go home. Her head thumped, in the same rhythm as the demolition happening. Thud, thud. She sat at the bar, nursing a glass of iced water, and lazily flicking through her socials on her phone.

"I'm so glad Siddarth sacked your shitty ex." Charlie slid onto the seat beside her and leaned forward with her elbows on the edge of the bar.

Elle closed her eyes. "Yeah."

"What a fuckwit, saying those things to you."

"I don't really want to talk about it." Elle swallowed.

"Actually…" She paused. No, maybe she didn't want to discuss this. It was so embarrassing.

"Yeah?"

"When he said those things, I couldn't believe I'd ever been his girlfriend. Like what was I thinking?"

Charlie's eyes glinted. "He must've been good in bed. Skills like that are wasted on an asshole."

Elle hummed. She'd never talked about this to anyone because who could she talk to about this? None of her friends had understood what she'd seen in him. Several of them had been pleased when they'd broken up, having said that many times. Of anyone in her life, then or now, Charlie might actually understand.

"Oh God." Charlie elbowed her and laughed. "Was he actually good in bed? I was kidding. Assholes like that are usually too selfish to be any good in the sack."

"Um, it's complicated." Elle was sure she was bright red. She must be, given the way her cheeks burned, and even her nose felt hot.

"Yeah?"

"He liked to…" She paused and glanced at Charlie who had an impassive look on her face, like she would just wait until Elle was ready. However long that might take.

"He liked to be tied up and spanked, and I liked doing that." Her admission was barely a whisper.

"Oh." Charlie's eyes widened and she bit her bottom lip as if she were holding back a giant grin. "Asshole out of bed, total sub in bed. That makes a lot of sense."

"It does?"

"Yeah. I've met a few people like that. It's almost as if the more power they have in life, the more they like to give that up in the bedroom. They seem to love the power games."

Elle breathed out in an unsteady rush. "Yes. He was such a dick to me, and honestly, I thought that was okay because it's not like my family are much better, and then he let me take control during sex. I loved that part, and I—"

"You were willing to ignore all the red flags to get what you wanted."

"You make that sound like a transaction." Elle didn't understand it herself, but that didn't feel quite right.

"Isn't all sex?" Charlie shrugged.

Elle swallowed. "Not for me." She couldn't look at Charlie as she suddenly realised what she'd just admitted. It wasn't fair either, because for a long time, that was exactly what they'd had; a transaction. Sex after Charlie's show to benefit them both with no emotional involvement.

"Sometimes the benefits aren't worth it. I'm glad you dumped him."

Elle's mouth dried up completely. Could she admit that she'd been so pathetic and desperate for attention that he'd dumped her? No. It wasn't worth losing Charlie's respect. "It was a long time ago. I'm different now."

"Hey, no judgement from me. I've always learned my lessons the hard way." Charlie smirked and suddenly everything was okay with the world again. The little smirk and the cocky glance settled Elle's stomach and she tried to smile.

"Right. Change is good, I suppose."

Charlie's little grin turned into a big smile. "Yeah, but no one likes to be reminded of their past mistakes in such a brutal fashion."

"Oh my god, yes." Elle wanted to bash her forehead on the bar as Charlie nailed the way she felt.

"It must be a nice petty satisfaction to have seen him get sacked."

Elle chuckled. "Does it make me a bad person that I enjoyed watching Siddarth tell Campbell that he was over his sexist crap, and he could fuck right off?"

"Nah, that was pretty spectacular. It must have been a while coming."

Elle sighed. "It can be quite hard to sack an employee." Now she had her own employees, she knew it was tricky to sack someone. Either they had to go through a long and involved disciplinary process or pay them to leave.

"It's why Beth keeps most of our dancers on contract." Charlie shrugged. "I mean, most of the people who dance here aren't really doing it for the money. It's a side hustle, or just for the fun of it, with the bonus of being paid for their time and getting costumes sorted out with Ace."

"Ace's costumes are incredible." Elle had recently learned that Ace was responsible for all the costuming at Seraph's.

"We are unique here because Beth pays for the costumes out of Seraph's main budget."

Elle frowned. "That's different?" She had no clue how it usually worked.

"Yes. Most dancers own their own costumes. A lot of people make them to save money because a whole outfit can get quite expensive. Dancers like working here because we have such a huge collection of different costumes and they can be freer with their choreography."

"That makes sense. I'm starting up a collection of items that I rent out to people who want to dress a house for sale.

There wasn't much need for it when I first started the business; it was tricky to sell houses when people were in lockdown, but now, people are starting to sell houses again." The demand had surprised her until someone mentioned that people had been stuck inside their houses for more than a year and likely wanted a fresh outlook. Having global interest rates at all time lows had contributed to a rising market too, so people were trying their best to present houses to get the most of the current gains. Elle was merely making the most of the current situation.

Charlie beamed at her. "What a brilliant idea."

Another flush of heat spread over Elle's face at Charlie's praise. "Thanks."

"Are you uncomfortable with being told you are good at something?" Damn Charlie for her perception.

"Um, yeah."

Charlie nodded. "I can see why … Never mind. So why interior design?" Charlie's quick change of subject only cemented Elle's grimace. Yes, her inability to meet her parent's high standards was exactly why she'd fallen for Campbell and stayed even after he'd continually shown her who he was when he wasn't begging her to tie him up. It'd taken a long time and a lot of reading to work out that his version of subbing and him being a dickhead out of bed weren't connected. Kinks weren't necessarily related to the way someone treated others.

"Design is about people, and how they belong in a space. I love figuring out how a client relaxes when they aren't at work, what colours they find soothing, how they move around their space."

"How about that!" Charlie grinned.

"What?"

"We have something in common, apart from…" Charlie leaned in closer even though they were the only two people in the room, "—great sex."

Elle didn't think her face could get hotter. Talking about work had been a temporary reprieve and now she flushed again. "Like?"

"Burlesque is all about entertaining people, making them happy. Your work might not be entertaining, but it makes people happy. Same same."

11

Charlie hadn't expected to find something in common with Elle's work. Maybe it was a bit of a stretch to say that they both made people happy, yet it fit, like one of Ace's corsets, perfectly crafted for her body. For all her chit-chat about how Seraph's was different because they let dancers share their collection of costumes, she wasn't very good at sharing. But then, she was a full time employee here, the only dancer with that status, so she ought to get a few perks.

"How long will that noise go on for?" After being told that the interruptions weren't going to be too bad, the builders had banged for an hour already.

"A couple of days."

Charlie nearly choked on her breath. "Days. What?"

"There are several walls to pull down before they can begin with the reconstruction. I talked to Siddarth about how to manage the whole build so we could keep Seraph's open. Most of the disruptions will be backstage, so the public won't know, and of course, the builders won't be here when Seraph's is open to the public."

"Most of the disruptions?" Charlie wanted to know which ones would be public.

"In the second phase, we'll be doing a few things to freshen up in this room. Mostly minor cosmetic things, like new panelling around the stage. That type of thing."

"Can we get new tables?"

Elle laughed. "I wish that was in the budget, but Beth wanted to focus on getting the back stage area more functional for the long term."

"I know that makes sense, but damn, some of our tables are fucked."

Elle nodded. "I've been thinking that most of them would be fine with a bit of a sand."

"Are you also a table expert?"

Elle shot her an odd glance. "Um, no. Though I used to do furniture restoration as a hobby a while ago."

"So you are a table expert?" Charlie loved the way Elle spluttered at her comment and she wanted to make her do it again. "Because most of them are too wobbly to use for fucking."

"For fucking?"

"Yeah. There's nothing like…" Charlie leaned in closer and whispered in Elle's ear. "…leaning over a table and being fucked. You'd do a good job."

"Me." Elle's reaction was completely worth it. It took her a moment of wide eyed staring before the corner of her lips curved upwards and Charlie had to hold in her grin. *Yes. Come on, Elle. Say it.* Be the sexy confident top that showed up occasionally.

"I do have a dildo that would work well."

Yes! Charlie grinned. "Ha. I knew you'd understand.

Unfortunately, there's only one table steady enough for the job."

"We'd better do something about that then." Elle's brown eyes sparkled. Just as Charlie was certain that Elle would touch her, she sat up straight and picked up her phone to dial someone. "Hey, Sam. I know it's been forever. ... I'm good. No, this isn't about the refit for Kensington. ... Are you still doing your classes? ... Awesome. Well, you know how you used to say that you were always looking for furniture to use in your classes? ... Yeah, I've had an idea that might be worth considering. ... Do you think there would be enough interest in a table restoration class? I'm doing a refit at a club and all their tables are rubbish. They don't have the funds to replace them, but I reckon they'd be able to pay you and all the materials if you ran classes that would get the tables fixed. ... Yes, it's a commercial business and yes, I know your stance on that." Elle laughed. "Of course there is a 'but'! You'll like this business. It's Seraph's Burlesque Club. ... Very queer friendly and they do dance lessons too so they are set up to run classes. ... Sure. Take your time. I'll send you an email."

Charlie's curiosity grew through the whole conversation until she almost burst with it. "What are you planning?"

"That was Sam. She runs a furniture restoration business that we use all the time for our clients. I met her when I did one of her courses and we've become friends."

"And you thought this Sam could use our tables for a course?"

Elle smiled. "Yes. Isn't that a great idea? Seraph's would provide the tables, the space, and the materials, and the students would refurbish all your tables. Chairs too if you wanted."

"I can see why Beth and Reiko and Yolande keep raving about you." Charlie could imagine a whole bunch of people happily sanding tables and fixing up the legs or whatever during the day, with Elle walking around keeping everyone on task with her commands. Hmm. What Charlie really wanted was for Elle to spread her over one of the tables and fuck her with the dildo, just like she'd mentioned. Spirals of heat spread over her skin and she tried not to squirm on the bar stool.

"They do?"

"Yes. It's become very tedious. 'Elle is so wonderful. You are going to love what she does with the place. She made me a model.'"

"Hey. What's the matter?"

Charlie sighed. "Nothing. I don't know. I shouldn't bitch like that."

"I didn't take it that way."

"Thank you." Charlie had meant it that way though and she didn't want to think about why it irritated her to have everyone tell her how great Elle was all the bloody time. She knew that Elle was awesome. If she was honest, she wanted to date Elle, not just fuck her sometimes.

"Do they really say that? It's very nice of everyone to have such a high opinion of me."

"Why do I sense you are going to say 'but' and make some excuse for why you aren't awesome?" Charlie was tired of the way Elle didn't have much confidence in her ability. "For fuck's sake, you run a whole design business. People are allowed to have high opinions of you and you should own that." Now she sounded grumpy when she was trying to tell Elle that she was valid and good.

"Um, thanks."

"I mean it. Own that shit. If I had your skills, I'd be telling everyone. That 3D model you made for Beth is fucking stunning."

Elle opened her mouth and Charlie pressed her palm against it. Charlie almost forgot what she was going to say as Elle's soft moist lips touched her skin.

"Don't you dare tell me that it was nothing. That model isn't nothing." Charlie pulled her hand away before she did something wild, like slide her hand around onto Elle's cheek and tug her closer for a kiss.

"Okay. Thank you. I'm glad that everyone liked it. It proved to be useful in figuring out the final design." Elle's cheeks had patches of colour on them, her light brown skin glowing under the bar lights. The background racket of the builders faded away.

"Can I kiss you?" It was easier than asking if Elle would go on a date with her.

"Not here."

"In my office. No one would hear us with the builders making all that noise." Charlie winked. She didn't expect Elle to agree, so when Elle picked up her glass of water, she tried not to slump on the bar.

Elle drained the glass of water, then placed it carefully back on the coaster she'd been using. She held out her hand.

"Shall we?"

It took Charlie a moment to realise that Elle had agreed with her.

"Yes." She grabbed Elle's hand, slightly cool from the glass of water, and slid off the bar stool. It was only a short walk to her office. Each quick step felt slow, like a chassé, because she was touching Elle's hand and she wanted to be in her office now. Not in thirty steps. Elle didn't talk until they were in Charlie's office.

"I can't believe I'm going to do this," Elle said.

"Why not?"

"It's not even lunch time—"

Charlie laughed so hard, she nearly choked on it. Eventually she managed enough breath to retort; bloody COVID ruining good jokes. "Since when does time have anything to do with sex?"

Elle waved her hand around the room. Her hair had started to come loose from her ponytail, and it gave her that wild look Charlie adored. "There are people all around us. I'm supposed to be working."

"And it's not even lunch time!" Charlie couldn't resist.

"Yes. And that. What am I doing?" The anguish in her voice made Charlie pause.

"Fine. I need to go home and sleep anyway. Text me when you are ready." The irregular thumps from the builders punctuated Charlie's grumps. She slung her backpack over her shoulder and grabbed her phone.

"Wait."

Charlie's heart skipped a beat and she turned to look at Elle.

"I'm sorry. This is really confusing." Elle waved her hand between the two of them.

"I'm tired. Grumpy. I have to be back here for my actual job at seven tonight. I need to sleep somewhere that isn't my office chair."

"Okay. Look after yourself." Elle nodded once, then left Charlie alone in her office.

If Elle was confused by this, Charlie didn't know what

she'd call her own feelings. She swayed between pushing Elle away and wanting to hold her closer. Forever. Charlie growled. Shit. Did she really want forever with a gorgeous interior designer who didn't believe in herself? Put like that and it sounded silly. Between her life at Seraph's and Elle's work, they'd never see each other. They wouldn't come home from work and lie on the couch, cuddled up, because Elle finished work just as Charlie started.

If Charlie was sensible, she'd hook up with a chef, or someone else in entertainment because at least their schedules would have a chance of matching. But she wanted Elle. More than she ought to. Somehow, sometime, Elle had stopped being one of her fun hook ups, and had started to become a friend as well. Elle challenged her. She made her feel real, and she never judged her for wanting the attention of an audience. Instead, Elle championed her work. She came to Charlie's shows. Charlie knew Elle had done extra work for Seraph's that she wasn't billing to Beth, and that both pissed her off because Elle needed to stop undervaluing herself and warmed her heart because Charlie couldn't help but hope that Elle did some of it for her.

She couldn't let her leave on such a grumpy note. Charlie dumped her bag and paced out of her office, moving around Seraph's until she found Elle with her head bowed over a table. The builder Siddarth was next to her with his head far too close to Elle's for Charlie's liking. A burning sensation built in her chest. Charlie made herself hang back and wait until they'd finished.

"Hey Elle. Can I have a moment of your time?"

"Sure." Elle walked towards her and Charlie had to focus her breathing to keep it regular as Elle's satin business shirt pulled across her tits as her arms swung gently at her sides. Charlie wanted to hold her tight and possess her. Crap. *Did she really want that?*

"Um, I wasn't kidding." Way to sound awkward, Charlie. "I need to go home and get some sleep, but do you want to catch up for a bite to eat tonight? Maybe once you are done for the day and before I have to be back here?"

A smile lit up Elle's face. "I'd love that. Text me, and please, get some rest."

Relief flooded Charlie's body with every muscle relaxing. "Okay. See you later."

See, there was nothing to be nervous about. Elle wasn't going to reject her attempts at furthering their friendship or whatever this was. Holding back a grin, she walked with a skip in her step back to her office. Her hamstrings twinged a bit. Hmm, she ought to do some stretches before bed, if she could be bothered by the time she got back to her flat. After grabbing her backpack from her office, Charlie bounded out the front door and jogged to the tube. She hadn't been this excited about a date—a fucking date—in ages. Where should she suggest they meet? Nothing too fancy. Somewhere that told Elle she was important, more than a friendly catchup, but not so fancy that it was intimidating.

Charlie ran her hand through her hair. This was why she didn't date. There were too many decisions to make, and all of them were based on what someone else might perceive. It was too hard. She wouldn't bother for anyone who wasn't Elle. Oh fuck, she was so screwed. So much for not being nervous. Her pulse raced and she couldn't exactly blame the lingering effects of COVID or the way she'd run to the tube for her lack of breath.

12

―――――

Elle leaned on the bar and grinned at Charlie. They'd eaten dinner together every single night this week, which had been weird on the first night when Charlie had left to come back to Seraph's for work. Elle had almost followed her, but she had emails to catch up on, so they'd kissed and parted without taking it any further. The kiss had sustained Elle all evening as she'd stared at her laptop and she had bounced into Seraph's to oversee the builders the next day. Generally, they'd avoided weighty topics, instead gossiping about Seraph's.

Walter and Steph were on a campaign to get Beth to let them have a cat in the flat they rented above the bar; they'd babysat Yolande's Captain and Bounce a while back and had loved being cat parents. Neither of them wanted kids, and Charlie took great delight in finding it ironically funny that Steph now wanted to be a cat parent when she'd been so adamant for so long that the bar, and all the guests, were enough for her.

Elle had gone home after each dinner to her own place and

dreamed of more time alone with Charlie, while Charlie had gone to work at Seraph's. Was it possible to have a relationship when they had such different work schedules? Was that what Elle wanted? Dinner together was nice, the kisses afterwards were even better, especially last night when they'd finger fucked each other in the alleyway behind the pub they'd eaten at. Elle flushed at the memory of rough bricks against her back, Charlie's rose perfume surrounding her, and her fingers slick as Charlie clamped around her. The undercurrent of lust never went away for her, but was it enough to sustain a relationship?

Now they stood beside each other at Seraph's and watched a bunch of keen queer artists sand down the old tables at Seraph's. Sam's class had sold out almost as soon as it had been announced. Each student would refurbish a table and learn a bunch of skills in the process, then they would have the opportunity to paint an original design on the top of the table, before it would get covered in resin and preserved with their signature. When the four weeks of the course were done, Seraph's tables would look amazing.

Sam was dressed in a stunning green gown that emphasised her height and when paired with sturdy boots, it was the perfect look for her as she walked around the room helping each of the students.

"This is amazing." Charlie tapped her fingers on the bar.

"Yeah. Sam is great." Elle had learned so much from her furniture classes and loved that she had a queer friendly environment where people could be themselves without judgement. It was a special gift to create a place with such openness and freedom, while the whole focus wasn't on who people were but on learning a new craft. Sam's furniture restoration courses had really helped Elle with her confidence and her business, and Sam's friendly teaching methods added to that sense of achievement.

"She really is. This whole class is the spirit of Seraph's." Charlie gasped. "Of course! Let me get Ben."

"Ben?" The IT guy? Why? She'd been away with the fairies and had missed something important, instead thinking about Sam and life and Charlie and whether it was possible to have a life together with Charlie.

"Yeah. Ben is a master at photography. He can take a bunch of amazing photos and we can put them on the club's socials."

"Make sure you ask the students first."

Charlie winked. "Yes, boss." Charlie's smirk sent a flash of heat over Elle's skin. "We are all about consent at Seraph's. Of course, I'll ask them all for permission before I do anything. I'd bet that most of them would want to be tagged in their own post anyway, so I'll need those details too."

"True." Elle smiled as Charlie leapt off the bar stool and marched through the room. She wore skinny jeans paired with a tiny crop top today and several of the students admired her as she walked past them. Pride filled Elle's chest with warmth. This was the person she was having sex with. The warmth disappeared immediately. Things were going well between her and Charlie, but there was one thing Elle wanted to talk about and wasn't sure how to mention. She wanted to be exclusive with Charlie. It would completely change their friendship. Did she want to take the risk that Charlie might say no? And if she did say no, could Elle continue being with Charlie? Or would it hurt too much knowing that she wasn't wanted by Charlie in the same way Elle wanted her?

"What's the matter?" Sam asked.

"The class is going well." Elle changed the subject.

Sam raised one eyebrow. "That doesn't explain the frown." She reached out and brushed her thumb between Elle's eyebrows and she rolled her eyes. Elle pushed Sam's hand away.

"It's…" Elle breathed in deep, not wanting to say 'nothing' when it was something.

"Let me guess. You have the hots for that incredibly gorgeous woman who was just here chatting to you."

"The hots? How old are you, Sam?" Elle chuckled.

"Well… It's true, though. I saw how your gaze tracked her across the room when she walked."

Heat bloomed on Elle's cheeks and she wanted to hide. "Everyone watched her. Not just me."

Both of Sam's eyebrows lifted, not just the one from before. "Darl."

"Fine. It's a bit more complex than a simple lusty yearning." Lusty yearning? Could she get any more cringe? Ergh.

Sam laughed. "Oh darl, you are in so much trouble."

"Trouble?"

"I remember your first class with me. You brought along an old chair and wanted to recover it because the material reminded you of someone you wanted to forget." Sam's eyebrow somehow got even higher. "It took me weeks to get that little titbit out of you. Shall we skip the awkward dance around the truth and you just tell me what is going on?"

Elle's stomach tied in knots, but the empathy on Sam's face made the decision easy. "Fine."

Sam smiled. "Good. Now tell me the problem, darl."

"Charlie and I have had a thing happening for a while—"

"What sort of thing?" Sam interrupted.

Elle sighed. "Why am I telling you this?" She knew though —she had no one else to talk about it with. Her brother wouldn't understand, and neither would Willow. She sure as hell wasn't going to talk to her employees or her parents, and many of her other friendships had faded away during the pandemic. Beth might understand, but her snarky teasing was a little much and there was the whole Charlie-works-for-her complication, and the fact that Beth was her client. Reiko was a good listener, she'd understand, but Elle didn't exactly have a close friendship with her yet. Again, Reiko and Yolande were her clients who might become friends one day if she figured out this thing with Charlie. It was too soon to talk to them, and they weren't exactly separate from the whole bloody mess.

"Because I'm a great listener."

Elle placed her hand on Sam's forearm and squeezed gently. "You really are. Thank you."

"So… Tell me about you and the smoking hot woman who is over there chatting to the equally hot Black guy. Is everyone here so stunning?"

"Yes." Elle wanted to cross her arms and hug herself, or shake out her hands, or something. Anything. Instead she twisted her hands together in her lap, just to put them somewhere. Sam kept waiting, her question hovering in the air, as if she knew she'd cave eventually.

"Okay, fine." She caved.

"Gees, you make it sound like I'm twisting your arm for juicy details." Sam grinned, her eyes twinkling.

"It's complicated, that's all."

"All of life is complex, darl. That's the joy of it."

Elle grinned. "Thanks for the two bit philosophy." She

sighed. "Okay. So Charlie and I used to hook up before the lockdowns, and we've recently reconnected."

Sam's eyes widened. "That is a little bit more complex than unrequited yearning."

"Yip," Elle said. "I think I want more. I really like her, you know."

"Darl." How could Sam get so much empathy into one word? "Have you told her this?"

"No. What if she only wants the same as always?"

Sam nodded slowly. "Tell me this. What is worse? Telling her how you feel and having her reject you, or not telling her and never knowing if she might feel the same way?"

"I don't know. Neither of those sound good."

Sam chuckled and kissed her on the forehead. "Good luck. I see someone wanting my attention."

Elle wanted to say something sarcastic but she couldn't, because as annoying as Sam was, she was also correct. Elle needed to figure out which of those options was worse. Could she be brave enough to face rejection?

13

Charlie ignored the beep of her phone as she carefully added a long wing in navy blue to her left eye with a stroke of her makeup brush. Tonight, Elle would be in the audience because she didn't have to work the next day, and Charlie was going to ask her to come home with her afterwards.

She wanted Elle in her bed; no more fucking in the hall-ways at Seraph's. She wanted to wake up next to her and take her time being kissed by her. It would be a test, to see if she actually wanted to be with Elle like that. A way to determine if these pesky feelings to spend more time with Elle were real, or just a symptom of her general dissatisfaction with her job and life and everything. She finished the other eye, then glanced at her phone.

Mum: Tom wants to meet you.

Her stomach lurched. Over the past few weeks, the press had forgotten about her and she'd started to settle back into work and life without the threat of the paparazzi hanging around. Charlie almost replied, 'well he can fuck off' but curiosity won.

Charlie: When?

Mum: Tomorrow

Charlie: I'm working in the evening. Lunch?

Mum: Yes. I'll talk to him and let you know where.

It was bound to be somewhere very exclusive and private. Somewhere special. An idea beckoned and she grabbed it. She could really do with a support person and there was only one person she wanted beside her.

Charlie: Can I bring my girlfriend?

Three dots appeared then went away, then appeared again. Charlie chuckled under her breath at the way Mum couldn't decide what to write. It wasn't really fair to tease her mum like this. She needed to keep Tom happy for their new project, and her mum needed the work a lot more than Tom did. Besides, family came first and Mum was her family. Tom was just some guy who'd donated sperm and paid for stuff. Charlie didn't know him.

Charlie: Ask Tom if it's ok first.

Mum: Will do

Charlie put her phone down. She needed to finish her face and put on tonight's wig and costume. It was an older one for tonight, one she hadn't worn in ages, and there was no point in letting it just sit around. Her phone beeped again. That was fast—she didn't want to think about how Mum had an answer from Tom already. It'd barely been a minute.

Elle: I'm here. This is weird.

Charlie: Come on back to my office.

Elle: Ok

A few minutes later, Elle walked into her office. "Oh, I'm sorry. I didn't realise you were getting dressed."

Charlie held her breath as she finished painting glue on her left nipple. If she laughed now, she'd shake and the glue needed to be precise to ensure the costume sat properly and only the bits that needed to stick stayed stuck. Costume failures weren't fun. She picked up the tassel and stuck it in place, holding it tight against her breast.

"Should I go?"

"You've seen it all before. Stay. Chat."

Elle's eyes widened, just as Charlie had hoped. Those gorgeous dark brown eyes were so expressive.

"You can help if you want?"

Elle stiffened for a moment and then the transformation came. Every single time this happened it was fucking glorious to watch. The moment when Elle stopped being timid and took control.

"Help get you dressed, or undressed?"

"Both if you like. Help me get dressed for work, and later, when I'm done, you can help me remove the final pieces of my costume."

Elle sucked her bottom lip into her mouth and Charlie nearly dropped the brush she'd been using for the glue. She put it down and waited to see what Elle would do. Elle stepped closer and traced her fingers up Charlie's arm, along her shoulders, and down her spine. She stopped just above the waistband of Charlie's sweatpants. They weren't glamourous—like, at all—but they were practical, warm, and easy to remove when she needed to finish the bottom half of her outfit. With a single step, Elle came closer to stand right behind Charlie. It would be so easy for Charlie to lean back a fraction and rest her back against Elle's body. Before she could, Elle shifted.

The fabric of her shirt scraped against Charlie's bare skin, but it was the shape of Elle's tits against her back that made her skin alight with glorious heat. Elle stretched up, her tits pressing as she dragged herself higher. Charlie held her breath, waiting, and when Elle kissed her on the nap of her neck, Charlie sighed. Not with contentment, with the relief that came from finally getting Elle's lips on her skin. She'd barely teased her at all, and Charlie was panting for more. The gentle scrap of Elle's teeth made her moan.

"Quickly. I have to be on stage in an hour."

Elle giggled against her skin. "An hour. That's hardly a challenge. I can make you come in less than five minutes."

"Please." Oh, this was the version of Elle that she never wanted to give up. The force of want slammed into her and she nearly pushed Elle away.

Elle wrapped her arms around Charlie's waist and Charlie covered them with her own.

"You'll have to leave my tits alone. The glue needs to dry."

Elle huffed out a hot breath on her neck and Charlie shivered. "So sexy."

"You know it." The laugh caught in her throat as Elle bit gently on the tendon of her neck, then dragged her teeth over her shoulder blade and down one side of her spine. It'd probably leave a red trail. Yes. She wanted it, wanted it visible in the photos Ben would take tonight, a keepsake of this stolen moment with Elle. Elle nuzzled the small of her back, and with a wriggle, she pulled her hands away from under Charlie's, leaving Charlie holding her own stomach.

Heat grew in Charlie's core to match the wet between her legs. Her breath came shorter and shorter and for a half-second she almost panicked as her scarred lungs begged for more air, before she let herself free. Let herself just feel the way Elle's mouth caressed her lower back. The cool air on her overheated skin as Elle pushed her trackpants lower and lower. The smoothness of Elle's lips as she kissed her naked arse cheeks. Elle bit her—not hard—just hard enough to make Charlie squeal.

"Hey."

Elle soothed the area with soft kisses and then continued to trail kisses lower, all the way down the back of her left thigh almost to her knee. Every touch left Charlie wanting, panting, needing more. And when Elle finally stopped playing with her —toying with her—and slid her hands up the inside of her thighs to touch her exactly where she needed it, Charlie moaned in relief.

"You like that?"

Charlie rested her hands on the bench and leaned forward slightly. "Yes." It came out all desperate and breathy. "Do it again."

"Patience."

"But you said less than five minutes," Charlie whined, needing Elle's fingers and mouth on her right now. She arched her spine, opening herself up more, and the cool evening air was fresh against her soaking wet labia.

"I do like a challenge." Elle slid three fingers inside her, and a thumb into her arse. The round heat of that invasion was a beautiful contrast to the slick heat of Elle's fingers inside her and she leaned further forward to extend her position. Elle pumped that hand slowly, leaving Charlie needing more.

Charlie pressed backwards against the pressure of Elle's hand. It wasn't enough.

"More. Please." Charlie wasn't above begging right now. She needed to come. Now.

Elle used her other hand to play with Charlie's clit and Charlie rode her hands hard. Rocking and moaning as the delicious tension built and built in her body. She was so close. So bloody close.

"Please."

Elle pinched her clit at the same time as she bit her arse and Charlie came in a rush of pleasure at the sudden pain. She cried out, pumping her hips against Elle, crying out the wild release of emotion in a jumble of words.

"Oh my God. Fuck. Fuck. You are so amazing. Fuck. I love you."

Elle stilled and so did Charlie.

"I love this." The last pulses of her orgasm rolled through her body and she started to realise what she'd said. "You are amazing, Elle. Thank you." If she kept babbling, perhaps it would go unnoticed.

"I know." Elle kissed her on the same spot she'd bitten, a soothing kiss that took away the last of the heightened touches that had sent shudders flooding through her body. Elle pulled her hand away and stood up. Charlie turned around to thank her with a kiss. The wide eyed expression on Elle's face almost stopped her and she leaned forward to rest her forehead against Elle's instead.

"Did you mean it?" Elle asked.

Charlie didn't know—maybe this was love, or maybe it was just the best fucking orgasm of her life—and a fresh wave of panic set in.

"That you are amazing. Yes. I meant that." Plausible deniability; wasn't that a thing?

Elle cleared her throat quietly. "Okay. I'll see you afterwards."

"Yes. Please." Charlie held Elle's chin between her finger and thumb and tilted her head up for a kiss. She poured everything she couldn't say into the kiss. It was too early to admit love, wasn't it? She'd said it in a fit of passion. It wasn't real. Was it? "I'd better keep getting ready. Steph will get you a drink."

"Sure. I need to go and wash my hands." The flat tone of Elle's voice was a sledgehammer to her gut. It was obvious she'd heard Charlie's blurt and now it sat awkwardly between them. There was only one thing for it—ignore it, pretend it hadn't happened.

"I want to see you again after my show." Charlie kissed Elle once more—a thank you and an apology, then slowly turned back to the mirror. In the reflection, she saw Elle square her shoulders before nodding and walking out. It would be fine. Charlie's stomach twisted; it had to be embarrassment, not panic that she'd told Elle the truth before she even understood it herself. Surely Elle would understand. Charlie didn't do love. Her fingers slipped when she tried to pick up the pot of glue and she grimaced; all she wanted to do was chase after Elle and tell her the truth.

Charlie did love her, probably, maybe, definitely. Yeah, she was in so much trouble.

14

Elle couldn't believe she'd just met Tom Scottridge and it had been as awkward as turning up to a picnic in hell with a cake in the shape of an angel. Charlie slipped her arm around Elle's waist as they walked out of the restaurant.

"I hope you didn't want dessert."

Elle shook her head. "Nah, it's fine. I'd rather be leaving than sit through another hour of that."

"I'm so sorry. Wasn't that dreadful?" Charlie cringed. Elle placed her hand over Charlie's and nodded.

"Yeah. It wasn't exactly what I'd expected when you asked me to have lunch with your parents."

"Tom is pretty intense."

Elle grinned. "Yes. The whole 'I'm on a special diet for my next movie. I'll have the Fish of the Day without garlic, onion, or citrus…' Like, the whole bloody dish was lemon and burned butter garlic sauce. Why not pick something that already had none of those things?"

"Then he wouldn't have gotten all the attention. That attitude should be enough to make the chef spit in his dinner." Charlie squeezed her arm tighter around Elle's waist.

"Charlie! I hope not. No one deserves that."

"Ergh. He's such a big star that the chef was probably happy to do a special order for him."

Elle giggled nervously. "I can't believe you talk about him like that. He's so famous."

"Apparently fame didn't make him less of a dickhead."

"Maybe it made him more entitled?"

Charlie breathed out loudly. "Yes. I mean, I know technically he's my … whatever and Mum is so thrilled to have him back in her life, but he's basically a brat. He made lunch so unpleasant. I'm really sorry I invited you."

"It's fine. I was pretty nervous beforehand. The idea of meeting a couple of famous people was quite overwhelming, but…"

"But they really showed you how they are just ordinary people with bigger egos?"

Elle laughed. "And I thought I was the cynic in our—" She stopped before she said relationship. Leading into this lunch everything was going so well between her and Charlie. There had been a little hiccup when Charlie had said those three little words, 'I love you', during sex last night and then had pretended she hadn't. And then they'd had more sex after the show without the same declaration.

Charlie had credited Elle with her best burlesque performance in forever. She'd laughed and invited Elle to help her prepare every night, because she'd strutted on stage and danced and it'd been amazing. It was all due to Elle, she'd said, then she had thanked her with multiple orgasms. Both that night and again in this morning as they cuddled in Charlie's bed.

Maybe Elle had misheard. She'd have to live with never knowing because she certainly wasn't going to bring it up. And now she'd suffered through an awkward lunch with Charlie's parents, which was a bit confusing. Wasn't inviting someone to meet your parents something people did after they said they loved someone?

"No, you are definitely the grumpy cynical one in this relationship," Charlie said, and Elle's heart skipped a beat.

They were in a relationship? Yearning for confirmation of that pulled at Elle's body and she leaned against Charlie.

"Does that make you the happy one?"

"Why can't I be sarcastic too?"

"Happy sarcastic works for me." This exchange skirted so close to the questions storming around Elle's brain. "Hey, are you working tonight?"

"No. We are closed on Mondays. I only told Mum I had to work so I would have a reason to leave early if it was awkward."

"You lied to your mum?" Elle could never do that. She'd been tempted on many occasions but believed that if she was to be different to her parents, she couldn't treat them like they treated her. They lied to her to suit themselves all the time, so she would never, ever, lie to anyone.

Charlie shrugged. "Don't you?"

"I wouldn't." More than that, she couldn't. She couldn't be just like them. Charlie moved away from Elle, and she immediately missed the warmth of Charlie's arm around her waist. Charlie stood in front of her on the footpath and rested her hands on Elle's shoulders.

"Elle, you are a grown woman. You run your own business. If a little white lie makes your life easier, just do it."

Elle's chest tightened. "Do you do that to me?"

"Sure. I mean, no."

"Sure?" Elle repeated Charlie's answer, stunned by it. "What the hell? How am I supposed to trust you now?" Elle saw Charlie flinch and she knew she'd overstepped, but what was she meant to do with that information? Did Charlie lie to her? How many times had she already lied to her? When? Her chest felt like it was getting crushed. This admission by Charlie had destroyed everything between them. There would be no more wondering where this might go, no more anticipation of kisses, and definitely no more glorious sex.

"You can trust me."

"You just admitted you'd lie to me if it made your life easier." She pushed Charlie's hands off her shoulders. "I can't do this. I was going to ask you to be exclusive with me, maybe work towards living together or something, but no. Not with someone who is loose with the truth."

Charlie's face went pale. "Wait. Let me explain."

"I think you've explained enough." Elle held her handbag tighter against her side and stormed off. She'd put up with endless red flags from Campbell, taught by her parents, and their continual lies as they altered their stories to suit themselves, that having the truth twisted was all she deserved. After Campbell had dumped her sad desperate self, she'd eventually picked herself up and learned her lesson.

Never again would she share herself with someone whom she couldn't trust and who didn't give her the same honesty that she gave them. She would never have an honest relationship with her parents—she was resigned to that—as much as she might want them to change, they were never going to be the parents she wished she had. Knowing that, and being aware of it, had helped her realise she didn't have to repeat the pattern. Campbell—for all his crap—had taught her a valuable lesson. She needed truth from a partner to break the pattern of her upbringing.

Until now, she'd viewed Charlie as an open, honest person. She didn't hide who she was; Elle knew she was one of several people Charlie hooked up with and she was okay with that because it was honest. There was no sneaking around, no pretence. But it was all a farce. Charlie only showed Elle whatever made life easier for Charlie. Elle's needs came second. It was the same old boring fucking story.

Elle marched with her chin held high. She refused to be trampled on again, refused to be taken advantage of, and used for someone else's gain, with no thought of her own feelings. She walked and walked, not paying attention to where she was going, with the conversation on repeat in her head, as if it were slowly drilling holes in her scalp.

Eventually she stopped and leaned against the edge of a fountain. The light spray of water in the late summer afternoon misted against the clammy sweat on her skin. Standing here, surrounded by Londoners busily going about their business, made Elle feel off balance. How could everyone just carry on like that while her life, her love, had collapsed around her?

"Hey." Charlie sidled up beside her. Had she followed her? Of course, she had, she hadn't fucking teleported here. Whatever, it was a wasted effort.

"I'm done." All the earlier passion had gone from Elle's body. There was nothing to say to Charlie. Whatever they had been was over. Over.

"I'm not." Charlie paused, her breath rasping lightly. "Please."

Heat prickled at the corners of Elle's eyes. No, she would not cry now. Later, maybe, when no one was watching. Not now, with Charlie standing beside her.

"Why is this such a big deal to you?"

Elle twirled around. "Are you fucking kidding me? Why is expecting you not to lie to me a big deal? Really? That's your question?"

"Yes. I would never lie about the big things."

Elle waved her hands, enraged by Charlie's illogical statement. "How do you decide what is big and what is small? It's better not to lie at all."

"Isn't that a bit unrealistic?" Charlie closed her eyes. "I'm sorry. I'm not helping, am I?"

"You think?!"

"I just want to understand."

"Why? Why should you care? We just fuck sometimes, Charlie."

Charlie's face went bright red. "The problem is that I do care. I—" She shifted from one leg to the other. "I don't want to hurt you."

All the air around Elle seemed to disappear. What had Charlie almost said?

No. Elle lifted her head higher—it didn't matter if she was going to say she loved her. "It's a bit late for that." Elle fell back on sarcasm to cut through the thickness around them. The whole world faded away, as if covered in a fog, and it was just her and Charlie standing beside a giant fountain of a naked woman. The mist from the water would've been romantic in any other circumstance. Right now, being damp just added another reason why she was fucking pissed off.

"Please. Help me understand."

Elle really shouldn't do this. She ground her teeth together to stop herself, but she was weak and she gave in. "You were right when I said I should tell my parents to piss off. They don't care about me. They lie to get what they want. Their image and our perfect family matter more than reality, and everything that happens gets twisted to fit the perception they want to convey. I can't be with someone who is comfortable with lies." Elle's heart pounded so hard, she could barely hear herself over the drumming of it against her chest.

"Oh."

"Yeah. Oh. Being sorry isn't enough, Charlie. I can't be with someone who doesn't respect the truth." She pushed away from the stone ledge and kept walking. She didn't have to look back to know that Charlie hadn't followed her. Why would she? It was hopeless.

Elle needed something that no one could possibly give: complete brutal honesty and no manipulation, no white lies, nothing that would remind her of the way her parents discarded her feelings to put themselves and their fucking image first. She had fought bloody hard to be valid and truthful to herself, and to make sure her own needs were met. She worked hard to know what she wanted. No one would take that victory away from her. Being alone for the rest of her life was better than forever wondering if or when someone was lying to her.

15

Watching the hurt on Elle's face cut Charlie like a steel blade. She had no clue how to fix things between them; and hadn't understood why a little throw away comment would result in a fight. Besides, like Elle said, it was too late to fix the hurt she'd caused. She'd already lied to Elle by pretending she hadn't blurted out that she loved her. She'd been too embarrassed—scared—to admit the truth, so she'd just slid around it and pretended it hadn't happened. Elle needed trust. Charlie kicked the stone ledge, imaging it to be Elle's fucking parents who'd hurt her over and over. Pain sliced up her leg from her toe. Why didn't Elle just leave? Toxic families didn't deserve continual forgiveness. They didn't deserve wonderful, giving, sarcastic, confident, clever Elle. Elle could create her own family.

Damn it. Charlie glanced down at her bloodied toe. No wonder it fucking hurt, she'd stubbed it in her fit of frustration. What kind of untrustworthy, uncontrolled person kicked a stone wall and expected to get away with it? Lucky she wasn't a ballet dancer who needed to stand on her toes; she could still dance with it cleaned up and neatly bandaged, hidden away under closed toed stilettos.

Charlie leaned over and scooped up some water from the fountain and splashed it on her face. The cool water on her skin helped clear her head. Unfortunately it didn't solve her problem. If she raced after Elle and admitted that she loved her, it would get thrown back in her face. It was impossible to believe with this timing. She'd have to show her instead. Fuck. How? All she knew was how to use her body to make people happy, and she knew—deep down—that sex wasn't enough in this situation. They already had amazing sex. As if Elle was going to let Charlie touch her or kiss her now, anyway.

What a bloody mess she'd made, literally and figuratively. Charlie already let herself get closer with Elle than with anyone else. It'd been over a month since she'd even thought about hooking up with someone who wasn't Elle. When she'd realised that, it was the beginning of understanding that she loved Elle. She loved the way she was so thoughtful, and yet confident and bossy when they had sex. She loved the contrast of the way she considered someone's opinion at work, but once she had made a decision, nothing would change her mind.

Shit, shit, fuck. Elle had already made up her mind about Charlie. This was doomed. It wouldn't matter what Charlie did; Elle had already decided it was over. And she was so beautifully stubborn that Charlie couldn't see how to fix this mess. Charlie sat down on the stone edge of the fountain and closed her eyes. How had it come to this? Before the pandemic, she couldn't have imagined herself wanting to try and fix anything. She would've happily walked away, shrugging her shoulders casually, and found a different person to hook up with. She'd never bothered to guard her heart. She hadn't needed to. Emotions and sex didn't collide in her world; her body was her job, her joy, and she adored sharing it with people who appreciated her.

Somehow, Elle had managed to curl up next to her, entangled, and now her heart and her emotions were involved. Charlie didn't really know what to do about it; this had never happened before. How had love snuck up on her like this? She was defenceless against this ache in her heart, she hadn't known that she might need to protect herself from this hurt, because she'd never imagined falling in love with someone. Now that she had fallen in love with Elle—completely and desperately in love—it surprised her, in a being-slapped-in-the-face-without-warning kind of way, not in a comforting-warm-blanket way. How had she managed to fuck it all up before she'd even admitted the truth to herself?

"Excuse me, can you please take our photo?"

Charlie opened her eyes to see a random young woman staring at her. "Yeah, sure."

She jumped up off the fountain's edge and took the woman's phone, pointing it in the direction of the fountain and the woman who draped herself over the bloke standing next to her. They both grinned at each other as if being here together was more important than the fountain or anything around them. Charlie handed them their phone back and they thanked her before wandering off holding hands.

Must be nice to have that ease with someone else. She could have had that if she hadn't been too frightened to admit the truth of her feelings to Elle. What now? She had to do something, but how on earth could she convince Elle she was trustworthy? Elle—who guarded herself in ways that Charlie couldn't even imagine—needed someone who would hold her when those barriers were breached. Charlie ran through different ways she could do something to show Elle how she felt. She could give her something, not flowers, but something that mattered to Elle. Would a gift be enough? Elle wanted truth; it wasn't something you could brush off with a gift or a one-off gesture. Charlie had no ideas, or at least, no useful ideas. She could stand on her stage and declare her feelings. Shit, that made her pulse pirouette, and she was all light-headed, but would it be enough? It didn't feel like it was the consistent truth that Elle hinted at. Trust had to be earned, it couldn't be proven with one grand gesture.

She walked all the way back to Seraph's with her head bowed, her mind unhelpfully blank except for one stubborn thought. It was all over between her and Elle unless she could find a way to keep being there for Elle, to simply be her friend, to love her, and listen to her. She could do that. It would require being brave, less shallow, and she nearly sat down and cried.

She was just a shallow dancer who'd grown up around equally shallow actors; all her life was a stage, and she needed an audience more than she wanted to admit. The pandemic had made it bloody obvious that she was nothing much without people adoring her. The task of adoring and supporting Elle seemed impossibly difficult. She knew how to be adored, but not how to do the adoring. Charlie gasped—that was why it was exactly what she needed to do. She would find the necessary depth to be Elle's friend, companion, and hopefully partner and lover.

"Charlie. Fucking just stop already." Beth leaned against the doorframe of the newly finished warm up room. With polished wooden floors, and floor-to-ceiling mirrors on two walls, and a barre, it was almost twice the size of the old room. Of course, Elle had designed something incredible for Seraph's.

Charlie stopped pacing up and down the room. "What?"

"All that energy is exhausting. When did you last get laid?"

"Beth!" Charlie laughed at her boss, not wanting to admit that it had been four weeks. Four whole fucking long weeks. Ever since Elle had told her it was over, Charlie had thrown herself into being Elle's friend. One line from their argument had rolled around her head all month. Elle had wanted to be exclusive with her, and so Charlie—foolishly—had decided that she would do that. It was Elle or no one. This was the longest she'd ever gone without sex since she was, like, eighteen, and fucking hell, Beth was right. She was so full of uncontained sexual energy that it spilled out.

"Is everything on target for tomorrow?" Tomorrow night would be the grand reopening extravaganza and Charlie had spent four weeks putting together an incredible program featuring almost everyone who had danced for them in the last five years.

"Yes." Charlie breathed in and out deeply. "There was one minor change to the program, but I emailed that to you an hour ago, so it just needs your approval."

"That's why I'm here. Are you sure?"

Charlie gulped. "No. But yes. I need to do it. We all need to do it. Seraph's is a family. I want to acknowledge everyone's role here." Charlie had suddenly realised that while she had a lot of people performing over the evening, she'd done nothing to acknowledge the support crew. Reiko, the kitty; Ben, the IT guy; the builders, and of course, Elle, whose design had transformed Seraph's. The most obvious changes were in the front of house—the new table tops were so artistic and incredible—but the best changes were the backstage ones. Everything made a lot more sense now.

"Even Elle? Did you clear it with her?"

Charlie grimaced. "Not yet." Her newly found emotional bravery … Well, it was a fucking joke because she hadn't found any of it yet, and the idea of asking Elle if it would be cool if she stood on the stage with the builders and all the staff at Seraph's while they all thanked her for the design and project management scared her. Kind of. It wasn't asking Elle to stand on stage that scared her. It was asking Elle to become part of the Seraph's family—with her. Together.

"I thought you two were friends." Beth smirked and Charlie wanted to growl at her boss.

"It's complicated."

Beth raised one eyebrow. "It's not. You just need to be brave and tell her how you feel."

"Stop being an interfering mother fucking hen, Beth."

Beth didn't flinch at having her employee talk to her like that—at Charlie's obvious frustration—instead her bloody smirk increased. "Oh, hi Elle. Was there something you needed?"

Charlie grabbed the barre and glanced wildly around the room, much to Beth's apparent amusement, given the huge grin spread across Beth's face. She felt faint and nearly sat down.

"Jesus Beth. Don't say that."

"Say what? Oh, you mean, I shouldn't talk about how you are in love with Elle and too scared to tell her? How you've spent a month hanging around her like a moth to a lightbulb, clinging desperately to all scraps of attention from her. How you stop everything whenever someone mentions her name and listen, as if you could just hold her once more by hearing someone else talk about her. You mean like that?"

Charlie nodded, misery pooling in her stomach until she thought she might gag on it. "Have I been that obvious?"

"Yes." Beth's face softened into empathy. "Love is a complex thing, Charlie. It's okay that it takes you a while to figure it all out."

"I don't need to work it out. I already know I love her. But she needs someone who isn't me. She needs someone she can trust, who isn't pathetically needy for attention, and who has some actual substance." Charlie had spent four weeks trying to figure out how she could be enough for Elle, not just someone who always told the truth, but someone who had enough emotional depth to be strong enough in herself to be there for Elle.

For four weeks, she'd seen Elle every day, making sure she was at Seraph's at the same time Elle would be there. They'd talked. Not about anything important, just day-to-day stuff, and Charlie had soaked up every little snippet. She really— really—wanted to kiss Elle, more than anything, especially when she bit her bottom lip while she was thinking about something. Charlie wanted to sooth that lip, kiss it better, and tell Elle how incredible she was.

"Charlie. You are a performer. You already have the bravery to get up on stage and show people who you are; you just need to believe it yourself."

"Sure." Charlie knew Beth wouldn't understand. No one did, hell, Charlie barely understood what she needed. She wasn't keen on the idea that she needed to change to be enough for Elle, this wasn't about that; she needed to find more of her real self, more depth, more substance. She wasn't looking to change, just to be more.

"I'm here for you when you need to talk about it."

"I know. Thanks, Beth, you are a wonderful friend."

Beth nodded. "Let me know if you need any more budget for tomorrow night. We want it to be a proper showcase."

The change in subject jerked at Charlie. "Um, sure. I think we are fine. Ace will be here later with new costumes."

Charlie had choreographed the opening dance to be a tribute to her all-time favourite burlesque dancer, Josephine Baker, with all the dancers for the night lined up in 1920s style burlesque outfits with banana skirts that Ace had spent two weeks creating. The old kick step had been such fun to practice together with Yolande at one end of the row and herself at the other, and everyone else in the middle. Jack and Dan would open the dance, dressed in top hats and tails—all removable, of course—and take the role of the old theatre masters. They'd written a hilarious script. She'd even managed to get her mum to convince her producer to bring along a couple of cameras, so the whole show could be recorded on proper cameras, not just the one they'd bought at the start of lockdowns to do dance classes with. Elle's redesign of Seraph's was going to be celebrated in the only way Charlie knew— with a big loud extravagant show that would make everyone in the audience feel amazing.

"Excellent. Now go tell Elle how you feel and get laid. All

this—" Beth waved her hand, "—pent up energy is bloody distracting."

Charlie could only shake her head at Beth's advice. She didn't want anyone else. Only Elle. Charlie swallowed as, for the first time in her life, she had a ridiculous thought. Sex would have to wait until she could be with Elle. Nothing else would satisfy.

16

Not eavesdropping was probably sage advice, but when Elle heard Beth mention her name, she hadn't been able to stop herself from listening. It was obvious that Beth was pretending she was there, especially when she started talking about how Charlie was in love with her and then Beth accused Charlie of being too scared to tell her.

Elle wanted to scoff—she couldn't imagine Charlie being scared of anything—and then Beth kept going, saying how Charlie clung desperately to all scraps of attention from her. Really? Charlie had been hard to avoid over the last month, and it didn't matter how many times Elle had to remind herself that Charlie was cool with lying to her, she couldn't seem to stay away from her. And then, surprisingly, Charlie had agreed with such anguish in her voice, as if it physically hurt her to admit she cared.

"I already know I love her. But she needs someone who isn't me. She needs someone she can trust, who isn't pathetically needy for attention, and who has some actual substance," Charlie said, and Elle's heart broke all over again. She wanted to march in there and tell Charlie not to be ridiculous. She had substance and bravery. Charlie, quite literally, stood on stage and took off most of her clothes. Okay, she did seem to need an audience admiring her, but that didn't mean she was shallow. She was a performer, and a performer without an audience was what? Oh. Elle suddenly understood how hard the lockdowns must have been for Charlie; and an uncomfortable flood of prickly heat—akin to guilt—filled her body.

She'd been so busy working on her business that she'd never given a thought to how Charlie might not have coped without her stage. Missing her audience didn't make Charlie shallow, just lonely. But it wasn't any of those thoughts that dominated. All of those things were temporary, flighty, fragmented thoughts that quickly faded. Charlie had said the one thing that Elle had convinced herself she'd misheard. Charlie already knew she loved her. Elle walked away, stunned, and unable to remember why she'd walked down this hallway in the first place. What should she do now? Was love enough to overcome their argument about truth? Had Elle overreacted to Charlie's little white lie comment? No. And the association with whiteness and harmlessness was something else annoying to throw into that messy pile that drove Elle towards a future alone. She could rely on herself. What she needed to do was ignore Charlie's belief that she loved her and get on with the job. Finish this contract with Seraph's and pay off the debt to her parents. Then she could move on with her life. Alone. Yeah—she sighed—if only it were that easy.

"Elle, did you get those light fittings?" Siddarth stood on a ladder in the middle of the stage and she blinked. *Focus, Elle, get the job finished.* If she concentrated hard enough, she could

—almost—ignore the way her heart had skipped hopefully when she'd heard Charlie declare her love.

"Sorry, I got distracted." She rushed back down the hallway, past Charlie's office and into the store room to grab the box of lights she had been supposed to get. By the time she'd come back to the main room, and slid the box onto the elevated wooden stage, Siddarth had moved the ladder and was beginning to hang the next lighting bar.

"That's not quite the right spot." Elle stepped back and looked critically at the stage. "It needs to be more to the right. Come and look."

Siddarth climbed down the ladder and jumped off the stage to stand next to her. "Where?"

"See how the three light bars at the back are evenly spaced. The next row needs to fill the spaces, and then the single one at the front sits just behind the curtain and slightly lower than the row at the back."

"Yeah?"

"Hold on. I'll get up there and show you." Elle walked around to the stage door, then up onto the stage. She clambered up the ladder and waved to Siddarth. "You need to imagine how each light bar will get used by the stage technicians, so they can hang whatever type of lighting they want. The placement has to be right, so they can all be seen from the front of the stage." She leaned slightly backwards to demonstrate what she meant to Siddarth and wobbled a bit. Elle grabbed the ladder but it was too late. She had no time to react before she hit the stage floor with a thump that shoved all the air out of her lungs. Everything went black.

Charlie heard the screams and ran towards the stage automatically. A group of people were huddled around a ladder up on the stage, and Siddarth was pacing along the edge of the stage on his phone.

"Is she conscious?"

"Yes." Ben half-stood. "How far away is the ambulance?"

"Don't move her. They said that."

"Who is it?" Charlie swung herself up onto the stage and shoved Ben to the side. "Elle. Oh fuck. Elle."

Elle lay on stage, with her arm bent at a strange angle. She was moaning slightly and her eyes kept fluttering open and shut. Charlie threw herself onto the stage floor beside her, gently stroking her hair out of her face.

"Tell Charlie I'm okay." Elle's voice faded in and out.

"I'm here, Elle. I'll always be here for you." Charlie tried to keep the rising panic out of her voice. Nothing in her life had prepared her for this; for seeing the love of her life, crumpled and broken on the floor. She threaded her fingers through Elle's unbroken hand, holding her gently, while she cradled Elle's face with her other hand. All she wanted was to comfort Elle and keep her safe until the ambulance came. Where were they?

"What is taking so long?" Okay, so much for holding back the panic. Her voice rose and she had to fight it to focus on soothing Elle.

"Soon." Someone's answer was enough—it had to be enough. Charlie continued to murmur to Elle.

"Hold on tight, my beautiful Elle. It's going to be okay. I promise." She'd do everything she could to make sure that was true. "It will be fine. The ambulance will be here soon."

"Charlie. I'm fine. I'll be okay." Elle had to be in so much pain. Her breath was short and ragged.

"Move away from the patient. Thank you." Two paramedics knelt on the stage beside Elle. The younger Black woman asked Elle a bunch of questions, and then gave her something to breathe in.

"This will help with your pain. That's a nasty break."

The other paramedic, an older grey-haired East Asian man, made efficient work of putting Elle's broken arm in a temporary support. "Please move out of the way."

Charlie found it impossible to let go of Elle's hand, and it wasn't until someone put their hands under her armpits and pulled her backwards, that she did as she was asked. "I have to go with her."

"Yes, we can take one person with her."

"Run and get your phone, Charlie. I'll follow with any other stuff you both might need." Beth's practical advice dragged Charlie back to the real world.

It would probably be months before she'd be able to sleep without seeing Elle crumpled on the stage floor. Charlie ran to her office, sprinting through Seraph's, her blood pumping around her body, grabbed her phone, then rushed back to Elle. The paramedics and the builders were slowly carrying Elle off the stage. Seeing her lying prone on a stretcher was the absolute worst. If Charlie had thought her heart was injured when Elle had told her their relationship was over, it had nothing on seeing Elle like this. She followed the paramedics through the bar and outside into the ambulance. At least, during the ride to the hospital, she was allowed to hold Elle's hand.

"I love you, Elle." There was no indication that anyone, except the young paramedic, had heard her.

"Elle. Please open your eyes. We need you to stay alert now." The paramedic focused on her job and in any other circumstance, Charlie would have thanked her for the simple acceptance of their relationship.

"Tell Charlie I'm okay," Elle croaked, then closed her eyes again.

"I'm right here, Elle."

The paramedic reminded Elle to keep her eyes open, to stay awake until the doctors had examined her. Charlie's lungs hurt, they burned as if she had been climbing all 193 steps at Covent Garden station, and she realised that she hadn't been breathing properly since she'd first seen Elle. She focused on slowing down her breathing; she'd be no use to Elle if she passed out too. In through her mouth, slowly out through her nose. Breathing like this—opposite to dance training—helped calm her heart rate. It'd been years since she'd needed to do this; it was a trick she'd learned as a child when she had stage fright.

"Stay awake, Elle. Please." Charlie leaned closer and kissed Elle on the forehead. It was the most gentle touch, almost not there, because she hadn't wanted to hurt her anymore. Precious Elle with her neck in a brace and her arm in a support tied across her chest.

"How far?"

The paramedic glanced out the small window beside her. "Maybe five minutes. She's doing really well."

"Thank you." Charlie wanted to believe the paramedic more than anything in her life. Elle had to be okay because Charlie had an important confession to make. Being in love with Elle had crept up on her slowly, from being her favourite hook up before the fucking lockdowns, to the one person she missed the most while stuck in her house, and now ... Now that everything was open again and life could find a way to move past the pandemic, Charlie had grown to love their time together until it had evolved into actual love. She loved Elle. Completely. Fully. In a way that she'd never loved anyone else. Charlie was here, stuck beside her while she healed, and then, Charlie would tell her how she felt.

"Charlie?" Elle's quiet raspy whisper plucked Charlie's heart strings.

"I'm here, my love. Always." Charlie cradled her unbroken hand and pressed gentle kisses to her knuckles.

"I'm sorry for fighting you."

Charlie's mouth tasted like salt, and she realised she was crying. "Elle, it's going to be okay. The doctors will fix your arm."

Elle closed her eyes again and the paramedic spoke again to keep her alert. The ambulance made a sharp turn and Elle flinched as she shifted on the bed she was strapped to.

"Tell Charlie I love her and I'm sorry." Those glorious words slurred a bit.

"There's something wrong." Charlie tapped the paramedic on the arm. It was unnecessary as she'd already moved and was shining a light into Elle's eyes.

"Stay with me, Elle. We are almost there."

Elle groaned.

"Nearly there. That's good. Keep your eyes open." The paramedic didn't look away from her task. "She has a concussion and the pain meds are starting to make her sleepy. We need to keep her alert until we arrive, just in case."

"Just in case, what?"

The paramedic ignored Charlie's panic, somehow keeping

a calm tone. "This drowsiness is normal with the pain meds. Keeping her alert is a precaution, that's all. It doesn't mean anything." The reassurance did nothing to stop the way Charlie felt.

If Elle said she loved her while she was injured like this, did Elle believe she wasn't going to make it? No. Stop thinking like that. Elle was in safe hands with this calm competent paramedic. She would make it and they'd be together forever. Charlie just had to convince herself that everything would be okay.

17

Elle was bored. She'd been out of surgery for twenty-one hours; not that she was counting or anything! She was definitely counting. Every two hours, a nurse came into her shared room to check her. They'd given her plenty of pain medication, so her arm didn't hurt at all, and her vision had cleared up enough that she could flick through her phone for an hour or so before she had to rest again. This bed wasn't that comfortable, and she wanted to go home to her own bed to rest. Surely they didn't need to keep her here for much longer. It was only a broken arm and a mild concussion.

She didn't really remember the fall; she'd been on a ladder at Seraph's and had stretched out to show someone—Siddarth —something and had lost her balance. She was so … annoyed with herself for being so incompetent. What kind of interior designer couldn't climb a ladder? She closed her eyes for a second and mentally kicked herself. At least this setback wouldn't stop the job from being finished. Seraph's was almost complete and she had faith that Siddarth and his team of builders—especially since he'd sacked Campbell—would get the job done before the grand opening in a few hours. She was great at her job. She'd planned this one and it was on target. A little accident shouldn't bash her hard fought confidence like that. She refused to let it.

"Hey." Charlie entered the room and Elle grinned. It was so great to see her lover here. Damn, she'd missed her, and she tipped her head a little hoping for a kiss. "How are you?"

"Great."

"Must be some good drugs then. You are smiling as if you are keen to see me."

"I am. Why wouldn't I be?" Elle had almost no memory of her accident, mostly the searing pain in her arm, and a comforting notion that Charlie had stayed with her. She recalled a tenderness in the way Charlie held her hand and simply just stayed with her. Elle wanted Charlie to look at her the same way forever. She didn't want the frown which flashed over Charlie's face momentarily as she squared her shoulders.

"Are you sure you are okay?" Charlie's tone was tight and Elle didn't understand why?

"Yes. I mean, I'm not perfectly fine, obviously, since I have this." She nodded towards her arm, all wrapped in the cast they'd put on after surgery to realign the bones.

"Um, so..." Charlie paused. "Do you want me to stay?"

"Yes, absolutely." Elle wanted more moments with Charlie's tenderness, more of the gentle touch of her fingers when Charlie had wrapped them around her hand and stroked her hair out of her face, comforting her when pain threatened to take over. All of Elle's doubts over the last month had fled in those foggy moments after her accident.

"I'm sorry." Sorry for letting a small argument blow up and ruin everything. They could've had the last month together if Elle hadn't panicked. She still hated the idea that Charlie might lie to her, that wasn't going to change in a hurry, but she might have taken the time to listen to Charlie rather than push her away without a chance.

"Don't apologise, please. You didn't mean to fall off a ladder and hurt yourself, although if you keep planning to do dangerous things, you'll have to give me some warning. My heart can't cope with seeing you injured."

"You meant it all, didn't you?" Elle hadn't dreamed all those lovely things Charlie had told her on the ride to the hospital. She really did love her; it hadn't been something Elle had misheard. It was real.

Charlie—finally—leaned over the bed and brushed a soft kiss to Elle's forehead. "Everything. I promised I'd never lie to you ever again, and I meant it all. I love you, Elle."

Elle closed her eyes. Could it be true? "Oh, that's amazing."

"I'm here for you, Elle, as long as you need me."

Warmth and happiness spread through Elle's body and she wished she could pull Charlie into a tight hug. She just breathed in her rose perfume, dragging it down deep into her lungs, as if she could keep it there forever. Charlie kissed her head again.

"I mean it. Please don't scare me like that." Charlie pressed her cheek against Elle's cheek and whispered. "I love you too much to see you hurt."

"Charlie." Elle's mouth felt weird—probably all the medicine she'd been given—making it hard to form the words she really needed to say. "I'm sorry I didn't trust you. Being in love with you scared me so much, and it was easier to be mad at you."

Charlie kissed her, a soft peck on the lips, before she sat up. "Aren't we a pair? I blurted out my feelings accidentally, and then I was too scared to admit it. I want to be enough for you."

"You are. I just wish I was brave enough to be with you." It must be the drugs the hospital had given her because Elle was blurting out everything she'd stored up inside her. She didn't care; she'd been holding this for too long, and she wanted to be with Charlie more than anything.

"You are brave enough. I'm the scaredy cat, not you."

"Says the person who gets up on stage in front of all those people. I'd never do that."

"And I'd never run my own business. You are the most amazing person, Elle, and I only hope that I'm going to be good enough for you one day."

Elle coughed. "I quite like you as you are. Good sounds a bit boring."

Charlie grinned and kissed her again. Still too gentle.

"I won't break."

"What?"

"You can kiss me harder than that. I'm not going to break."

Charlie raised one eyebrow, and with that single movement, Elle knew everything was going to be just perfect.

"What are you talking about? You did just break."

"And the doctors fixed me in surgery. Did I tell you how great everyone has been?" Shit, Elle closed her eyes as her brain caught up to what she'd just said.

Charlie grinned. "Great drugs, at least. Have a sleep. I'll be here when you wake up again."

Elle let the darkness surround her, anchored to Charlie by her warm grip on her hand.

Time meant nothing in a hospital, it dragged at snail's pace, every minute taking longer than the one before. Elle cracked open one eye as one of the nurses asked her to wake up and ran through all the usual checks. Again. She'd been here long enough to be bored with the routine, which must mean that she was well enough to go home.

"What's the time?"

"Five in the evening." Had Charlie been sitting here for the past two hours? Longer? Had she slept through some of the nurse visits? Not knowing the answer made her doubt herself. Maybe she wasn't ready to be discharged?

"What day is it?" Elle needed to know how long she'd been here. How much time had she wasted lying here?

"Saturday." Something was important about Saturday. Why couldn't Elle remember? Her head ached.

"The doctor will be past on his evening round soon."

"Will they discharge Elle?" Charlie asked the nurse and Elle hoped they would. She wanted a shower, and to spend the evening on her couch watching a movie. It was just a broken arm and a slightly sore head, nothing that required all this attention. They should give the bed to someone who needed it more than her.

"Let's see what the doctor says and we can take it from there." Well, that was fucking informative. Elle waited as the nurse ran through all her checks. It was hardly fair to be annoyed at the nurse who was doing a good job. The public health system here had a few faults, but at least she would go home without spending anything, which wasn't something that could be said for other countries. She couldn't imagine the type of stress that a broken arm in the USA might cause someone. Imagine falling off a ladder, then going bankrupt because of medical costs. It sounded dystopian. On that scale, she'd much rather lie here for free, vaguely annoyed, for as long as the system took to sort out what was best for her care.

"Everything looks great. How is your pain?"

"Fine."

The nurse smiled. "Excellent. We'll have you back dancing soon."

Elle glanced at Charlie who looked like she was going to explode in giggles. "Um, thanks."

Charlie waited until the nurse left the room. "I suppose they assumed that since you came here from Seraph's."

"Yeah." Elle suddenly connected things. Saturday. Seraph's. "What about the grand opening tonight? You'd better get going. You'll be late." If it was already five in the afternoon, Charlie needed to be there now to get everyone organised to be on stage for the eight o'clock opening dance.

"It doesn't matter."

Elle gasped. "What do you mean it doesn't matter? You've worked for a month putting this line up together and all those dance practices with everyone. You can't miss it."

"I can. I'm not going without you." Charlie leaned back in her chair and placed her hands behind her head in a pose that Elle could only call; fake casual. The tension in Charlie's pose contrasted with the way she was attempting to look relaxed and casual. Elle bit her lip as she realised something. Charlie wasn't lying to her by pretending to be okay with staying, she was being brave and putting aside her own needs to put Elle first. Wow. People didn't do that for Elle, like ever, and it made her really uncomfortable, which wasn't exactly normal. Was it?

"I want you to go."

Charlie shook her head. "No. I love you. I'm not going to leave you here, bored and in pain, just to go and dance in a burlesque show."

"But—"

"No, Elle. I said I'd be here for you, so here I am."

Elle squinted at Charlie. Apart from the determination in her eyes, there was something else happening. Charlie had an odd expression, like she was holding back emotionally, and the notion tugged at Elle.

"There's more, isn't there?" She was pretty sure this wasn't anything to do with her own issues because why would Charlie look awkward over Elle's inability to let someone put her first? "Something else is the matter, more than just your determination to miss tonight for me."

"It's nothing." Charlie dropped her hands to her lap and sagged in the chair, then she lifted her head slowly. "No. That's a lie and I'm not doing that anymore."

"So it's … something?"

"Um, I'm not really a fan of hospitals." Okay, not what she expected at all. Elle almost shrugged except her arm hurt when she started to move her shoulder.

"I don't know many people who are."

"I had COVID. Last year. I spent ten days in hospital, so yeah, I mean, I love hospitals because I'm alive thanks to them, but I'm not so keen to be in one again."

"I'm so sorry." Elle reached out with her healthy arm and touched Charlie on the shoulder. "You don't have to stay if you are uncomfortable. I'll be fine."

"I do have to stay."

At that moment, Elle realised the truth. Charlie loved her enough to miss the grand opening she'd been working on, and she loved her enough to stay here with her in hospital even though it reminded her of her own hospital stay. Their argument about honesty meant nothing. Elle had overreacted because Charlie had just shown Elle the true meaning of love.

"Charlie." Elle had to tell her before she burst with it. Charlie really loved her and it was the most incredible gift anyone had ever given her. "Look at you. Look at how strong you are, and brave."

"What?"

"Thank you for staying with me."

"Of course I would stay. I love you."

Elle knew it was time to take her own advice and be honest. "And I love you. So very much. Wanting to be with you, and only you, scared me and I argued with you rather than admit my feelings."

Charlie's cheeks turned pink. "Pesky fucking feelings." She stood up and kissed Elle firmly on the mouth. Elle knew, with a certainty that she hardly ever felt, that she had found her forever person. She kissed Charlie back with everything she could, moaning and wanting more. Her healthy hand tangled in Charlie's hair and she wanted to drag her impossibly closer.

"Yes." The word was lost in their kiss. A loud cough sounded from behind them and Charlie leaped backwards, leaving Elle's lips bare and cool without her touch.

"I've reviewed your paperwork and you can be discharged now. You'll need to come back to the day clinic in a couple of days for an assessment." The doctor didn't look up from her notes while she made her pronouncement. "The nurse will remove your cannula, then you are free to go." And with that, the doctor left the room.

Elle grinned. "If the nurse is quick, we'll still make the grand opening tonight."

"Elle. No. I'm taking you home to bed."

"Promises, promises…"

Charlie grinned. "I fucking love it when you are like this. So confident and sexy." She winked. "I also love it when you worry too much and when you fuss, and when you finally make a decision and no one can change your mind."

"And I love your cocky confidence, the way you command the stage and get an audience eating out of your hands. You have so much inner strength and depth." Elle knew Charlie needed reassurance, that she was worried about being shallow, and it was easy to do because Elle knew the truth. Charlie wasn't shallow or needy. "There is no correlation between performing to an audience and the way you conduct your life. I know I overreacted when you told me to lie to my parents, and I'm so sorry. I let my issues get between us and I shouldn't have done that."

"If it matters that much to you, it matters to me as well."

Elle smiled. "I love you, Charlie. Now, where is that nurse? I need to get out of this hospital."

Charlie leaned over Elle's bed and just as Elle thought Charlie would kiss her again, Charlie hit the call button. "That should help move things along a bit faster."

"And then we can go to Seraph's."

"Are you kidding me? No, we can go home and I'll look after you."

Elle sighed. "It's just a broken arm. I want to celebrate with you."

"Seriously?"

"Yes, I'm serious. I want to go to Seraph's tonight. We've both worked hard. Let's enjoy that together." Elle could rest and heal later. This was important to Charlie.

"If it means that much to you, then let's do it."

"Doesn't it mean a lot to you too?" Elle couldn't understand Charlie's reticence.

Charlie sighed. "Yes. But you matter more to me than work, or adoring audiences."

"I can be your adoring audience. Just like the first time we met." Elle's face burned with heat at the memory of Charlie tipping champagne down her leg and into her mouth.

"That can be arranged. I've never done that trick with anyone else. It's yours and yours alone."

18

Charlie stood on the stage at the end of their grand reopening extravaganza. Her mum was in the audience seated next to Elle, but thankfully her famous father hadn't turned up. Most of the crowd were long term regulars and the artists who'd created the tables. All the contractors and builders were present, as well as the friends and family of the crew at Seraph's. She'd updated everyone on Elle's health on the group chat they had for their main crew, and everyone had been thrilled that Elle was being discharged. Reiko had said she'd make sure Elle was comfortable during the show and Charlie had been able to jump up on stage and run the show knowing Elle would be looked after.

"Let's give a huge thank you to all our dancers tonight." Charlie introduced them all as they walked on the stage and bowed alongside them as the audience hollered and clapped and wolf-whistled. The noise buzzed in her veins. There was nothing like this feeling; well, maybe one thing. The way her heart swelled when Elle said 'I love you' was better than this.

When the noise died down a little bit, Charlie thanked all the dancers again and they filed off the stage.

"Tonight is only possible because of a few special people. Ben, our stage manager and IT person."

Ben poked his head around the edge of the curtain and waved to the crowd before disappearing again. "He's not great at being in the spotlight. Much better at turning the spotlights on us!" The crowd laughed.

"And we'd all be lost without our kitty, Reiko. Let's hear it for Reiko." Charlie pointed in her direction and Reiko waved to the audience quickly. "And of course, our security, Walter, and bar manager Steph." The audience clapped again.

"Seraph's would be nothing without our wonderful Beth. She's the boss around here and is the best type of boss. She treats everyone at Seraph's like we are her family. Everyone, Beth."

Beth walked out on stage wearing an incredible tight fitting electric blue knee length gown in a latex wet-look fabric that shone under the lights. The top of her prosthetic leg was visible over her boots. She bowed to the crowd; once a dancer, always a dancer, then took the microphone from Charlie.

"Thank you. The nights at Seraph's would be boring without our incredible MC, The Gloved Gatsby. The loudest cheers should be reserved for her!" The audience went a little wild and Charlie felt herself blushing. It took several minutes before there was enough quiet for her to speak. She'd practiced this with Beth but hadn't expected this level of applause.

"Sorry, boss. I think you are wrong. I'm not the one who deserves the loudest cheer. There is someone much more deserving."

"Me? Why thank you." Beth bowed in an exaggerated fashion and the audience loved it.

"Everyone is here tonight to celebrate the grand reopening of Seraph's Burlesque Club." Charlie didn't have to look out at the audience to know that Reiko should be guiding Elle to the side of the stage. "Yes, I know we didn't technically close our doors during the refurbishment, so opening is a little bit of an overstatement. To all those who came here to be entertained while we had no tables, thank you."

"If you are planning to celebrate the people who stood around without tables, then—" Beth paused, as they'd planned. "—then you'd be right. Our guests are our most important people. Thank you everyone for supporting Seraph's."

Charlie waited for the audience to quiet down again. "Who loves the new décor? I'm quite the fan of the new tables myself."

"Obviously. You keep mentioning them!" The audience roared at Beth's comment.

"Because they are freaking amazing. Our thanks go to Sam who corralled a collection of artists together as they created the incredible artworks you'll see on each table. Can you believe these are the same old tables that we've always had at Seraph's? Sam's class refurbished each table, then created art for you all to enjoy."

Beth nudged her. "You really love those tables."

"Well, I have it on good authority that they are sturdy enough now for…" Charlie bent over and shook her tits, then cleared her throat dramatically. The audience catcalled her. Perfect!

"The tables are great, but my favourite part of the refit are the new lights above the bar. Aren't they super funky?" Beth's comment had the audience turning around and cooing at the new fittings.

"And that brings us to the most important part of the evening. I'd like to introduce two very important people. Our builder, Siddarth Jain, and our interior designer, Elle Denbigh-Yadav."

When Elle walked onto the stage beside Siddarth, Charlie's chest swelled with pride. *This was her girlfriend. Look at her.*

"These are the people who deserve the biggest applause." Charlie spread her arms wide in their direction and Beth clapped. The audience cheered, loud and energetic, and Charlie couldn't help herself. She walked the few strides over to Elle and kissed her. Not a polite kiss on the cheek, but the kiss she'd wanted to give Elle for months. A tender adoring kiss filled with all the love she felt for Elle. She brushed her hair gently off her face as she kissed Elle with all her heart. Elle tensed for a short while, then seemed to forget they were on stage at Seraph's and melted into the kiss. Her cast was hard between them, an ugly reminder of her accident, and Charlie took more care than normal. Eventually the incredible volume from the crowd seeped through the buzz in her ears and she straightened up.

"Elle. Thank you for creating a gorgeous space at Seraph's."

Siddarth took Beth's microphone with a grin. "Do I get a kiss like that too?"

The crowd laughed. Someone started chanting, 'kiss, kiss' and soon everyone joined in.

Charlie couldn't help it. "What do you think, darling? Should we invite Siddarth to join us for a threesome?" The crowd roared, loud enough to lift the roof, and Charlie almost missed Elle's whisper.

"He's cute, but I don't want to share you with anyone."

Siddarth laughed. "Fair call. If I was lucky enough to be sleeping with either of you, I wouldn't want to share either."

"Thank you everyone for a wonderful night. You've been a fantastic audience. Seraph's only exists because you guys are here. I hope we've been entertaining." Charlie nodded to Ben and he closed the curtain, hiding them from the audience.

"Why do I put up with you?" Elle's dark brown eyes were dancing. "I can't believe you kissed me in front of everyone."

"Can't you?"

"You are lucky that I love you, Charlie."

Charlie grinned so much that her cheeks hurt. "Come home with me. I want to look after you and help you heal."

Siddarth laughed. "Is that what you call it?"

"Come on, Siddarth. Let's grab a drink." Beth tucked her arm onto Siddarth's elbow and they walked off the stage, leaving Charlie and Elle alone. Well… As alone as anyone could be with only a curtain between them and a crowd.

"What do you say, Elle, my love? Shall we stay for a drink and perhaps a fuck in the hallway for old times sake…" Charlie winked.

Elle smiled. "Yes please."

"Excuse me? I was joking. What about your arm?"

"My arm will be fine if we are careful. Let's celebrate." Elle's smile lit up her whole face and Charlie felt herself grinning like wild too.

"Have I told you how much I fucking love you?"

If you enjoyed this book, you'll love the next book in the Seraph's Burlesque Club series, SHOW QUEEN.

They're real life enemies, but online they're besties…

Seraph's Burlesque Club owner Beth Zendeli is too old to take any nonsense. She hustled to keep her club afloat through lean years and a pandemic, and she doesn't let her disability define her. But her perfect location has been sold, and the club is being evicted. The new owner is unreasonable, immovable and irritating. In desperation, she turns to the online friends she talks about plants with…

Property investor Liz Whitten has plans for the old building she's just purchased, and she's used to getting her way. But when she meets the leaseholder in real life, a chance statement reveals Beth to be Liz's online friend QueenB. Can she really evict a friend? Especially a friend who is so unexpected and fascinating in real life.

Liz must decide if profits and ideals matter more than friendship, or if it's worth taking a risk on love.

~

In case you missed it, the first book in the Seraph's Burlesque Club series is SHOW UP.

A fake date … a real secret

An invitation to her ex's wedding is the icing on a crappy cake for burlesque dancer Yolande. Her ex ghosted her just as they were about to take the stage for their neo-burlesque act. Yolande's friends at Seraph's Burlesque Club persuade her that attending will show her ex that she's moved on. She just needs a date.

Shy bartender Reiko has a secret, or two. She can't risk anyone discovering that her life as a penniless PhD student and bartender is a sham. And even though she's been in love with Yolande since forever, when Yolande needs a plus-one to save face at her ex's wedding, Reiko knows any fantasy of romance is just that - fantasy. Yolande will never notice the way Reiko looks at her.

When the drama of the wedding reveals a spark of attraction between them, Reiko will have to risk her fake identity for the hope of real love.

- found family
- fake dating
- friends to lovers
- only one bed

∾

Want a bit more sexy romance and to see what happens at Reiko and Yolande's wedding? The wedding is available as an exclusive bonus when you sign up for my newsletter.

ACKNOWLEDGMENTS

I pay my respects to the Wangal people of the Eora Nation, who are the traditional owners of the land on which this book was written.

Thank you to Porcelain Alice and the team at Sky Sirens for all your help in my Burlesque research. "Burlesque dancers don't need to be good at dancing. They need to be good at entertaining," Porcelain Alice.

Thanks as always to MV Ellis, Lina, and the rest of my writing buddies, Charity, Dianne, the Lesbian Campfire group, and the Word Count Warriors at RWAus.

Ali, Marie, and Kait have been an excellent support crew for this series. It was a long, occasionally messy, road and they were there for me as we all navigated a difficult situation together.

AUTHOR NOTES

While this book is set in London, I wrote it from Australia. Writing a post-pandemic world where everyone is vaccinated is a type of contemporary fantasy, especially given the timing of when I wrote it (early 2021). For the most part, I've tried to keep the pandemic out of the story, and only allude to the impacts on the characters.

NHS Charities Together (https://nhscharitiestogether. co.uk/) is a federation of 240 charities that all focus on supporting England's National Health System. It came to prominence during the COVID19 pandemic when the 99 year-old Captain Tom Moore raised over £30 million for them by walking laps of his garden.

ALL BOOKS BY RENÉE DAHLIA

Thanks for reading SHOW UP. I hope you enjoyed it. Reviews can help readers find books, and I am grateful for all honest reviews.

Thank you for taking the time to let others know what you've read, and what you thought. If you write a review for SHOW UP and email me with the link, I will send you a free copy of the second book in the series, SHOW OFF. My email is renee@reneedahlia.com.

If you'd like to know more about me, my books, or to connect with me online, you can visit my webpage www.reneedahlia.com and if you sign up to my newsletter, you can grab a free book.

Twitter https://twitter.com/dekabat
Facebook https://www.facebook.com/reneedahliawriter/
Instagram https://www.instagram.com/reneedahlia_author/

You've just read a book in my Seraph's Burlesque Club Series.

Contemporary Series: Seraph's Burlesque Club

1. Show Up (ff with bisexual heroine)
2. Show Off (ff with bisexual heroine)
3. Show Queen (ff)
4. TBA Duo of Novellas (mm)

Contemporary Series: Kapow!

1. Out of Her League (fm with bisexual characters)
2. His Buxom Beauty (fm)
3. Craving His Spotlight (mm)
4. Her Pregnant Rival (ff)

Contemporary Series: Farrellton Foster Family

1. Betrayed (fm)
2. Forbidden (fm with bisexual characters)
3. Liability (ff)

Contemporary Series: Margaret River TV: Boxed Set

- Homage (fm with bisexual heroine)
- Uplift (ff with bisexual heroines)

Contemporary Series: Merindah Park

1. Merindah Park (fm)
2. Making Her Mark (fm with bisexual heroine)

3. Two Hearts Healing (fm)
4. Racetrack Royalty (fm)

Contemporary Series: Rainbow Cove

1. His Christmas Pearl (fm)
2. His Christmas Pride (mm)

Historical Series: Great War

1. Her Lady's Melody (ff)
2. Her Lady's Fortune (ff)
3. Her Lady's Honor (ff)
4. His Lord's Soldier (mm)

Historical Series: Bluestockings

Prequel: The Shipwrecked Earl's Bride (fm with bisexual hero)

1. To Charm a Bluestocking (fm with bisexual hero)
2. In Pursuit of a Bluestocking (fm)
3. The Heart of a Bluestocking (fm)